BEAUTY FOR ASHES

MARIO DESEAN BOOKER

BEAUTY FOR ASHES

DEDICATION

Copyright © 2025 by Mario DeSean Booker, Ph.D.**

All rights reserved. Except as permitted under the United States Copyright Act of 1976, no part of this publication may be reproduced or distributed in any form or by any means, or stored in a database or retrieval system, without the prior written permission of the author.

First Edition

Written by Mario DeSean Booker, Ph.D.

Edited by FaLessia Booker, The Editing Expert. www.falessia-booker.com

Published by: Punny Girl Books

ISBN: 979-8-9999707-3-2

Scriptures quoted from the King James Version (KJV) are used by permission. All rights reserved.

For permission requests, contact falessiabooker@gmail.com

It is forbidden to use or reproduce any part of this book, whether graphic, electronic, mechanical, scanned, or digital. This includes photocopying, recording, taping, or retrieving information from any storage system without written permission from the author, except

for brief quotations within critical articles. However, this book may be quoted in academic papers with proper citation.

The author has attempted to properly credit all sources used in this work. If any credit is missing, please let the publisher know so it can be fixed in future printings.

ACKNOWLEDGMENTS

To the women who transform brokenness into beauty—

This story belongs to every sister who has walked through fire and emerged refined rather than consumed. To those who chose forgiveness when revenge felt justified, those who extended grace when bitterness seemed easier, who stood in faith when circumstances screamed defeat.

To the women who understand that true strength isn't measured by the absence of scars, but by the willingness to let those scars become sources of healing for others. To those who know that sisterhood transcends blood relations, creating families bound by shared struggles and mutual triumph.

To the mothers raising children from foundations they're building while healing from wounds they never deserved. To the wives who discovered their worth wasn't determined by broken vows or failed marriages. To the friends who learned that authentic love sometimes requires difficult conversations and uncomfortable truths.

To the prayer warriors whose intercession moves mountains and the quiet heroes whose faithfulness sustains communities. To those who refuse to let their past dictate their future and who understand that God's mercy creates new beginnings from the ashes of what was destroyed.

You are seen. You are valued. Your story matters.

This book is written in honor of your courage, your resilience, and your unwavering commitment to rise above circumstances that were meant to bury you. May you recognize your own strength reflected in these characters and find hope in their journeys toward wholeness.

You are more than conquerors, beloved daughters of the Most High, and inheritors of promises that exceed your wildest dreams.

This is your story. This is your song of victory.

PROLOGUE: MIDNIGHT REVELATIONS

To the Almighty God, whose grace carried me through seasons of doubt and discovery—You took my scattered thoughts and wove them into purpose. Every word written flows from Your abundant mercy, every character's transformation reflects Your redemptive power. I am nothing without Your guiding hand.

To my beloved wife and editor, whose unwavering belief in my voice gave birth to this work—thank you for seeing beauty in my broken places and for pushing me toward genres that once felt beyond my reach. Your editorial wisdom shaped every page, while your love sustained every difficult revision. Without your fierce faith in my calling, this story would remain locked in my heart.

To my mother, Emma Jean Booker—your strength became my foundation, your wisdom my compass. Every lesson you taught through word and example lives within these pages. The resilience you modeled through life's storms gave me courage to write characters who rise from ashes. Your love remains my anchor in every creative endeavor.

To my Godmother, Robin Simbler—your spiritual guidance shaped my understanding of divine purpose long before I recognized writing as ministry. Your prayers covered my path when I couldn't see the destination, and your unwavering faith in God's plan for my life sustained me through seasons of uncertainty. The woman of faith you helped nurture now speaks through every character's spiritual journey.

April McGee, your literary fire ignited something dormant within my spirit. I learned that authentic storytelling requires courage to excavate truth from comfortable fiction. Your influence permeates these pages in ways you may never fully comprehend.

Ericka "Nikki" Paschal-Martin, my faithful cheerleader—your enthusiastic support arrived precisely when my confidence faltered. Your ability to see potential where I saw only possibility kept my fingers moving across countless keyboards during seasons when surrender seemed simpler than persistence.

Cheryl Denise Givens, my sister in Christ—your prayers and prophetic encouragement reminded me that God's gifts demand stewardship, not burial.

Ashonte' Nuate Booker, my sister-in-love—you witnessed the earliest fragments of this literary expedition and declared with prophetic certainty that words would become my weapon against darkness. Your early recognition of my calling planted seeds that bloomed into this harvest.

Brianna "Bri" Barnett, my Zumba Mama and treasured friend—through years of laughter, tears, and unexpected plot twists, you remained constant. You transcend friendship categories, becoming family by choice rather than blood. Your encouragement danced through my discouragement, keeping rhythm when my spirit lost tempo.

To every prayer warrior who interceded when my strength failed—your faithful petitions created spiritual atmosphere where creativity could flourish. I recognize that solitary effort produces limited results, while community support generates breakthrough.

I stand today because countless others invested their hopes, dreams, and sacrificial love into my tomorrow. Their shoulders provided the elevation from which I glimpsed possibilities beyond my natural vision. This acknowledgment cannot adequately capture the depth of my gratitude, but it represents my humble attempt to honor those who gave before receiving, who believed before seeing, who loved beyond logic.

May this work honor your investment and glorify the God who orchestrates divine connections for purposes exceeding our individual comprehension.

With profound humility and thanksgiving…

Mario DeSean

The Call That Changed Everything

Three o'clock struck on Shaniece's bedside clock as the cellphone's shrill ring pierced through her peaceful slumber. Groggily, she reached across the Egyptian cotton sheets, her hand fumbling in the darkness until her fingers found the receiver.

"Hello?" Her voice carried the weight of interrupted sleep, confusion threading through each syllable.

Silence stretched across the line—not empty silence, but the kind pregnant with intention. Heavy breathing filtered through the speaker, accompanied by indistinct sounds that made her skin crawl with unease.

"Look, whoever this is needs to stop calling this number," Shaniece declared, irritation replacing her initial drowsiness. "This behavior is completely inappropriate and—"

A baby's cry erupted through the phone with such intensity that she jerked the receiver away from her ear. The sound pierced straight through her heart, awakening memories she'd spent years trying to bury.

Lord, what kind of psychological torment is this? she wondered, slipping her feet into designer slippers while wrapping herself in the silk robe that had become her evening armor—beautiful, yet protective.

The rain outside commanded her attention as she approached the window. Each droplet traced intricate patterns down the glass, nature's own artistic expression playing out before her eyes. Something compelled her to remain on the line, though every rational thought screamed at her to disconnect. This wasn't her usual response to prank calls, but tonight felt different—charged with significance she couldn't yet comprehend.

That infant's cry had unlocked chambers in her heart she'd sealed with prayer, therapy, and sheer determination. Suddenly, she was seventeen again, terrified and making impossible choices in Renee's grandmother's dusty attic. The makeshift procedure that had stolen not just her pregnancy, but her ability to conceive—a consequence that had shaped every relationship since.

How could anyone know? Who would weaponize her deepest wound?

Heat flushed through her body as old shame and regret bubbled to the surface. Tears began their familiar journey down her cheeks, mirroring the rain's descent outside.

"Don't call this number again!" she commanded before disconnecting with enough force to rattle the phone's cradle. Her knees buckled, and she found herself on the bedroom floor, emotions wracking her frame like a storm-tossed ship.

The phone's ring shattered her moment of vulnerability. Against her better judgment, she answered.

"Hello?"

"Do you know where your husband is tonight?" The female voice dripped with malicious satisfaction, followed by laughter that chilled Shaniece's soul.

The question struck like lightning. *Where is Dalvin?*

"Tell me about Dalvin! What do you know?" Desperation colored her words as she gripped the receiver.

"Please," the voice mocked before the line went dead.

"Hello? HELLO!" Shaniece's voice crescendoed into a scream as she hurled the phone across the room. The device crashed against the wall, its plastic shell splintering like her composure. Thunder rolled overhead, as if Heaven itself acknowledged her anguish.

"If you would like to make a call..." the automated operator's voice emerged from the broken receiver.

"Yes," she whispered to the empty room, "I do need to make a call. I need to know where the hell my husband is."

Dawn's Harsh Light

Morning sunlight filtered through her windows like divine grace seeking entrance to a troubled heart. Shaniece cradled her Belgian hazelnut coffee, the warmth barely penetrating the chill that had settled in her bones. Loneliness had become her constant companion—not the peaceful solitude she once cherished, but an aching void that no amount of success or material comfort could fill.

The telephone's ring interrupted her meditation. Her greeting emerged flat and lifeless: "Hello?"

"Good morning, sister! Isn't this a magnificent day? The Lord's mercies are new every morning!" FaLessia's voice bubbled with enthusiasm that seemed almost offensive given Shaniece's current state.

FaLessia—Dalvin's sister and Shaniece's spiritual opposite. Where Shaniece had built a billion-dollar empire through fashion and cosmetics, FaLessia poured her multiple degrees into running *God's Healing Hands*, a nonprofit serving their community's most vulnerable. Their philosophical differences created constant tension: FaLessia questioned why Shaniece didn't use her wealth for greater charitable impact, while Shaniece wondered why her sister-in-law wouldn't leverage her education for financial independence.

"Good morning, FaLessia." The response carried obligation rather than warmth.

As FaLessia launched into her daily recitation of blessings, church announcements, and gentle evangelism, Shaniece's mind wandered. *She talks endlessly,* she thought, regretting answering the call. The monologue might have continued indefinitely if not for FaLessia's inevitable question about Dalvin.

Dalvin Shaw—the man who'd once embodied everything she'd prayed for in a husband, now representing everything she needed deliverance from. Her family still spoke of him as if he walked on water, blind to the reality that he'd become the storm threatening to drown her marriage.

Her mother's wisdom echoed through memory: "Child, don't invest in what you can't afford to lose."

Why didn't I heed that warning? The bitter truth settled over her like fog. Now I'm trapped with someone I can neither keep nor release.

"Where's that wonderful brother of mine this morning?" FaLessia inquired with genuine affection.

Shaniece surveyed their empty bedroom—no evidence of Dalvin's presence, no indication he'd returned home the previous night. The familiar questions assaulted her spirit once again:

What have I done wrong? Am I insufficient as a woman? Have I failed to be attractive enough, spiritual enough, submissive enough?

The receiver slipped from her fingers as she collapsed to her knees, tears flowing freely. Part of her wanted to gather all of Dalvin's belongings and deposit them on the front lawn, to declare her independence and self-sufficiency. Yet she knew she wouldn't follow through. Hope still flickered despite overwhelming evidence that her marriage was beyond resurrection.

"Hello? Are you there?" FaLessia's concerned voice emanated from the fallen phone.

"I'm here—the phone slipped," Shaniece lied, retrieving the receiver while stepping onto her balcony.

The morning painted a picture of renewal: ascending sun, birds celebrating the new day, flowers opening to receive light. Nature's testimony of resurrection mocked her dying marriage. Then she spotted Dalvin's car turning into their driveway.

Her clock read 9:45 a.m.—he was just arriving home.

She couldn't share this humiliation with FaLessia.

"Actually, Dalvin's downstairs reading the morning paper. What prompted this early call?" she managed, draining the last of her coffee.

"You're always awake before sunrise," FaLessia observed. "Up at 6:30 am every morning, leisurely puttering around all morning until noon, until retiring for an early bedtime at nine. You're wonderfully predictable."

The word *predictable* pierced like an arrow finding its mark. Her greatest fear—being ordinary, boring, forgettable—had been casually confirmed.

"I maintain a disciplined, balanced lifestyle," Shaniece defended herself. "Perhaps you should consider a similar structure. Earlier bedtimes, avoiding late-night eating—it might address those dark circles and help with your weight management." The words emerged before she could stop them, dripping with a sass reserved for enemies, designed to wound as she'd been wounded.

Blow for blow. Pound flesh for pound of flesh. But she didn't intend to hit this hard.

"Well ... hen Dalvin's available, please have him call me. May the Lord bless your day," FaLessia responded quickly, her voice betraying hurt.

The conversation's abrupt end confirmed that Shaniece's verbal dart had found its target. FaLessia was probably crying now. A momentary satisfaction filled the void, but it quickly evaporated as footsteps approached.

The time had come to engage in a battle she'd already lost: the fight to save her marriage.

CHAPTER 1: THE GREAT PRETENDER

CHAPTER 2: LOVE HANGOVER

"Good morning, sweetheart," Dalvin announced as he approached Shaniece, attempting to press his lips against hers with the casual confidence of a man returning from an evening walk rather than an all-night absence.

She pivoted sharply, her hand connecting with his cheek in a swift, decisive motion. How dare he waltz in here at dawn, acting as though nothing happened, expecting affection after abandoning me through the night? Her arms crossed defensively as she positioned herself strategically between him and any escape route. This confrontation would happen on her terms—no retreat, no surrender.

"What's troubling my baby?" His fingers reached toward her face with practiced tenderness.

She batted his hand away with conviction. "What's troubling me? The question, Dalvin, is what's wrong with you? Disappearing until dawn, leaving your wife alone while you pursue whatever activities occupy your nights!"

Her composure wavered when she noticed his expression—amusement dancing in his eyes like he'd just witnessed something entertaining rather than faced his wife's righteous anger. Heat surged through her veins, transforming her light complexion into burnished copper.

"What's funny? I am a joke to you? My feelings are a joke, right? Our marriage? Oh no, it's me! I am the joke," she declared, stepping backward when he moved to embrace her. "So glad I amuse you," she shouted.

"I'm smiling because you're absolutely beautiful when you're concerned about us," he replied, his voice carrying honeyed persuasion. "It reminds me exactly why I chose you—your passionate heart, your devotion, the way you fight for what matters to you. These qualities make me appreciate you more each day."

His fingers found her hair, and despite every rational thought screaming resistance, she felt her defenses beginning to crumble. Something in his touch awakened the woman who still loved him, still hoped for restoration. As his arms encircled her, she detected his masculine warmth, but underneath lay something unfamiliar—a scent that didn't belong in their home.

"You smell different," she observed, pushing against his chest. "Like you've recently bathed somewhere else. We use Zest soap exclusively. This fragrance is Dove. Where exactly have you been? If you're going to cheat and then bath try humoring me and using the same soap we use at home. Like be smart about your dumb stuff, that is the saying right"

Dalvin exhaled heavily, his hand moving across his scalp—a gesture she recognized as his preparation for elaborate storytelling.

"Listen...I was handling business at the office until nearly three this morning. You remember the Davidson campaign we've been developing? Today's presentation determines everything. Afterward, the team went to The Hot Spot for stress relief."

"You visited that establishment?" Her voice carried disbelief mixed with hurt. "Apparently you've forgotten what awaits you at home." She gestured toward herself with renewed confidence. "All of this—everything a man could desire—and you seek entertainment elsewhere?"

"Baby, you are absolutely magnificent," he insisted, pulling her closer. "Every man I know envies what I have. Your beautiful eyes, your graceful size six figure, your intelligence—you're perfection, and I recognize exactly how blessed I am."

Despite her anger, Shaniece felt a flutter of satisfaction. He should recognize what he has. Don't be foolish enough to lose something this valuable.

"I'm a size five, not six," she corrected automatically.

"Regardless of size, I would love you at any number because I fell in love with your spirit, not measurements," he whispered, beginning to sway with her in his arms. "After drinks, Brian and I hit the gym—we'd consumed too many wings and needed to work off the excess. That soap you noticed was all they provided in their facilities." His chuckle seemed genuine. "My beautiful wife got worried about me. You're everything I need. I rushed home so quickly I earned a speeding citation, but being here with you makes it worthwhile."

His lips found her neck, igniting responses she thought anger had extinguished. Despite her mind's protests, her body remembered their connection, the physical bond that had sustained their relationship through increasingly difficult seasons. Her breathing quickened as familiar desire stirred within her.

What followed was passionate reconciliation—bodies speaking the language that words had failed to convey. In those moments, Shaniece allowed herself to believe in restoration, in the possibility that love could bridge the growing chasm between them. Physical intimacy had always been their refuge when communication failed, their sanctuary when trust wavered.

"That was incredible," she breathed afterward, still catching her breath. "You've never...we've never connected quite like that before."

"I wanted to show you how much you mean to me," he replied, his voice carrying satisfaction and something else she couldn't identify.

"You're making it difficult to focus on work today, but I have responsibilities," she murmured, reluctantly extracting herself from the tangled sheets and padding toward their bathroom. The shower's warm water washed away physical evidence of their encounter, though the emotional complexity remained.

Fifteen minutes later, she emerged transformed—professional, polished, wearing her ivory Armani suit like armor against the world's judgment. Her hair flowed freely around her shoulders, a small rebellion against the structured day ahead. She pressed a gentle kiss to Dalvin's seemingly sleeping form, gathered her briefcase, and departed for another day of building her empire.

The moment Shaniece's car disappeared from view, Dalvin's eyes opened, fully alert. He reached for the bedside phone with practiced efficiency.

"Morning, man," he greeted Brian casually.

"Hey, Diz. Davidson was seriously impressed with our timeline completion last night," Brian responded, clearly multitasking from his apartment.

"Excellent news. Landing this account could transform everything for us—real financial breakthrough territory."

"True, though you disappeared around eleven when Davidson suggested extending the evening. He sent you that message about joining them."

"About last night—I told Shaniece I worked late, then visited The Hot Spot, followed by the gym. If she asks, confirm that story."

Brian's laughter carried through the line. "Always got your back. Teach me your methods someday?"

"Understanding women requires recognizing their fundamental needs," Dalvin explained, moving toward the bathroom with casual arrogance. "Provide emotional validation, demonstrate attention when present, and maintain physical satisfaction. Master those elements, and relationships become manageable."

"Sounds straightforward when you explain it. I need better skills. Time to prepare for work."

"Call me later."

After Brian disconnected, Dalvin immediately dialed another number. "Good morning, beautiful. How are you feeling? Missing me already?" His tone carried an intimate familiarity that would have shattered Shaniece's heart.

Meanwhile, Shaniece approached their driveway and found Dalvin's vehicle blocking her usual route. Deciding efficiency trumped principle, she opted to drive his car instead. As she adjusted the driver's seat, a yellow paper caught her attention—a traffic citation tucked partially beneath the seat.

Opening the glove compartment to store it properly, the time-stamp stopped her cold: **11:39 p.m.**

He claimed this ticket resulted from rushing home this morning. But 11:39 p.m. occurred last evening, not this morning. Moreover, the location shows the far west side—nowhere near his office on the east side, nor the south side gym and club he mentioned.

The pieces of his carefully constructed story crumbled like a house built on sand. She sat motionless, staring at the evidence of his deception while her mind raced through implications. His story contained multiple impossibilities, geographic and temporal contradictions that revealed elaborate premeditation rather than spontaneous explanation.

Shoving the citation back into the compartment, she glanced toward their bedroom window where Dalvin likely continued his performance of innocent sleep. *Your story doesn't align with facts, and I'm beginning to understand the depth of your deception.*

She reversed from the driveway with deliberate force, tires protesting against the asphalt as her mind began calculating the true cost of loving a man who had perfected the art of beautiful lies. The morning sun illuminated not only the road ahead, but the growing clarity that her marriage existed on a foundation of carefully constructed illusions.

Lord, grant me wisdom to see clearly and strength to handle whatever truth I discover, she prayed silently, knowing that some revelations, once uncovered, forever change the landscape of a woman's heart.

CHAPTER 3: THE WOMAN BEHIND THE MASK

Highway to Heartbreak

Navigating I-77's morning traffic, Shaniece felt her vision blurring as unshed tears gathered like storm clouds. Heat flushed through her body—not the warmth of summer sunshine, but the burning sensation that accompanies deep emotional wounds. The isolation pressed against her chest like a weight she could barely sustain.

Marriage was supposed to be my sanctuary, she reflected, gripping the steering wheel tighter. *Love was supposed to heal, to restore, to make everything beautiful again.* Yet here she sat, questioning whether the man she'd pledged her life to even possessed genuine affection for her. *How could he claim to love me while entertaining other women? How could someone who truly cherished me cause such pain?*

The thought of Dalvin with another woman sent nausea rolling through her stomach. To escape the present anguish, her mind retreated to sweeter memories—particularly that first kiss that had sealed her fate.

Memory Lane: The Picnic

August heat shimmered off the pavement that long-ago summer day when they were still navigating high school's complexities. Seventeen and convinced they understood love's mysteries, they believed their feelings could conquer any obstacle. Dalvin had orchestrated an afternoon picnic with the meticulous planning of someone determined to create a perfect romance.

"Good afternoon, beautiful," he'd called out, bounding from his car with the enthusiasm that had first captured her attention. As his strong arms encircled her smaller frame, she'd inhaled his unique scent—a combination of cologne and something indefinably masculine that made her pulse quicken.

"Put down whatever you're reading and come with me," he'd commanded with playful authority that she'd found irresistible.

During the drive to their destination, the wind streaming through her hair felt like nature's own caress. She'd studied his profile—the way concentration furrowed his brow, how he bit his lower lip when focused, the dimples that appeared whenever he caught her watching him. In that moment, surrounded by summer's warmth and his undivided attention, she'd known with absolute certainty that she loved everything about Dalvin Shaw.

Their chosen spot had seemed divinely appointed: beside a gentle creek, beneath an ancient oak whose branches created a natural cathedral, adjacent to wildflowers that added splashes of color to their romantic tableau. Birds provided musical accompaniment while they shared food, laughter, and dreams for their future together.

"Those clouds look threatening," she'd observed, noting the darkening sky.

"Nothing's going to ruin our perfect day," he'd insisted with the confidence of youth. "Even if it does, I'll protect you from everything."

Nature, however, had other plans. The downpour arrived with sudden intensity, but the oak's canopy offered shelter while they huddled together beneath their blanket.

"I apologize for the unexpected weather," he'd murmured, stroking her face with tender fingers.

"This has been the most wonderful day of my entire life," she'd whispered back, meaning every word. When his lips found hers for that first kiss, she'd felt transformed—as though loving him had unlocked some secret version of herself that was more beautiful, more worthy, more complete than she'd ever imagined possible.

They'd remained there for hours, kissing softly while rain drummed overhead, creating their own private universe where nothing existed except their connection.

Return to Reality

Honking horns jolted Shaniece back to the present, where she realized she'd been weaving erratically through traffic while lost in remembrance. *I need Mama's wisdom. She'll know how to help me navigate this mess.*

Twenty minutes later, she arrived at her childhood home, tears streaming freely down her cheeks. Memories of running into her mother's welcoming embrace flooded back—those arms that had represented absolute safety, unconditional love, protection from every childhood trauma. She needed that sanctuary now more than ever.

"Mama!" she called out, rushing through the unlocked front door and collapsing in the living room as though she'd thrown herself before an altar seeking divine intervention.

Silence answered her plea. The house felt empty, devoid of the maternal presence she desperately craved. Disappointment settled over her like fog as she sank onto the familiar sofa, scanning a room that had remained unchanged through decades—family photographs chronicling happier times, furniture that had witnessed countless family gatherings, walls that had absorbed years of laughter and occasional tears.

For an hour, childhood memories provided temporary refuge from adult complexities. But eventually, reality intruded when her phone announced Samantha's call.

"Where on earth are you? I'm drowning here without my business partner," Samantha teased from her executive office.

"I was just about to call you. You're more than capable of handling Hermosa—that's why you hold the senior vice president position."

"We have the Vamp meeting in five minutes regarding the cosmetic line expansion."

"Handle the presentation yourself. Have Jessica document everything thoroughly for my review later."

"What's so important that you're missing crucial business meetings?"

"I'm managing personal matters at Mama's house. I need to discuss Dalvin with her."

"Hopefully she'll advise you to divorce that worthless man," Samantha declared bluntly. "He's constantly traveling, ignoring you, and entertaining other women. The evidence keeps mounting—"

"I don't need a catalog of his failures right now. Let me handle this situation."

"Give Mama my love. We'll continue our conversation later."

After the call ended, Shaniece decided to return to work rather than wait indefinitely. As she approached Dalvin's car, a neighbor's voice called out across the street.

Ms. Jenkins approached with the determination of someone carrying important information. A heavyset woman whose housedress and falling stockings created an almost comedic appearance, she nevertheless commanded respect as the neighborhood's unofficial information network.

"Child, what brings you to this side of town? Don't you live in that fancy district now?"

"I came to check on Mama," Shaniece replied politely, though internally preparing for an extended conversation.

"Your mama took Dina downtown for some business. You remember Dina—that girl who married Greg Maynard? Biggest mistake she ever made, though I shouldn't speak ill." Ms. Jenkins paused dramatically. "They had another terrible fight last night. All that chaos isn't God-ordained, you understand? Young folks today rush into marriage thinking about everything except the foundation that actually sustains relationships."

Here comes the sermon, Shaniece thought, though she recognized wisdom in the older woman's observations.

"Without love—real love, not just attraction or convenience—you have nothing substantial," Ms. Jenkins continued. "Money can't hold families together when hearts have grown cold."

As the conversation progressed, Ms. Jenkins revealed troubling details about the neighborhood drama involving Dina and Greg—financial disputes, infidelity accusations, violence, and questions about paternity that had attracted Child Protective Services. One detail caught Shaniece's particular attention: Greg had accused Dina of involvement with someone nicknamed "Diz."

Diz...Dalvin's college nickname. Surely that's not coincidence.

When Mrs. Ruth, her mother's neighbor, joined their impromptu gathering, the conversation shifted toward church attendance and spiritual matters before Ms. Jenkins diplomatically suggested they relocate for "adult conversation."

Arriving at Hermosa's headquarters, Shaniece parked in her designated space and checked her appearance in the rearview mirror. The reflection that stared back seemed foreign—successful on the surface but hollow beneath. At thirty-one, she commanded a billion-dollar empire yet felt disconnected from her own identity.

Who have I become? The question haunted her as she studied her features. Behind her polished exterior, she glimpsed something disturbing—a lost little girl cowering in darkness, abandoned and afraid. The realization struck like physical pain, forcing her to close the mirror and collect herself before entering the building.

Two security guards rushed to assist her—opening doors, calling elevators, their eager smiles masking the deference money commanded. *Amazing how wealth transforms people's behavior,* she observed, momentarily distracted from her inner turmoil by the exercise of power.

From her eighteenth-floor office, the city sprawled below like an intricate map where people moved like purposeful ants through their daily routines. The view usually provided perspective and satisfaction, but today it only emphasized her isolation.

"Glad you finally decided to grace us with your presence," Samantha announced, settling into the Victorian chair as though she belonged there—which, in many ways, she did.

"Make yourself comfortable," Shaniece replied with affectionate sarcasm.

"Already accomplished. I practically live here more than in my multimillion-dollar home."

After discussing business matters—the successful Vamp presentation and partnership details—Samantha turned her attention to more personal concerns.

"Now, what has Mr. Dalvin done this time?" she asked, settling back expectantly.

"Sometimes I feel like I'm loving someone who *can't* or *won't* love me back," Shaniece admitted, her vulnerability showing through carefully maintained professional composure. "Everything feels different now—wrong somehow. I don't recognize myself anymore, and I certainly don't recognize my marriage."

"Listen carefully," Samantha leaned forward with the intensity of someone delivering a crucial truth. "This isn't about *your* inadequacy—it's about *his* character deficiencies. You're experiencing what I call a 'love hangover.' You've been intoxicated by hope, by memories of who he used to be, by dreams of who he might become. But intoxication eventually wears off, leaving you nauseated and clear-headed enough to see the damage."

Samantha's analogy struck with uncomfortable accuracy. Shaniece had indeed been operating under love's influence for years, making excuses and maintaining hope despite mounting evidence of Dalvin's betrayal. Now, as clarity gradually replaced delusion, she faced a critical decision: continue the cycle of hope and disappointment or find the strength to pursue something healthier.

Lord, grant me wisdom to see clearly and courage to act according to Your will for my life, she prayed silently, knowing that some hangovers require complete abstinence rather than moderation.

The conversation marked a turning point—the moment when love's sweet intoxication finally gave way to painful but necessary sobriety. Whatever came next, Shaniece knew she could no longer pretend that hoping harder would transform her marriage into something it had never actually been.

CHAPTER 4: WHEN DARKNESS FALLS

The quartet moved purposefully down Barbados Drive, their friendship evident in synchronized steps and shared conversation. New Orleans weather defied seasonal expectations—summer evening air carried autumn's crisp bite, winds whipping with unusual intensity. Yet nothing could deter their monthly pilgrimage to Ché Pierre, where Renee' Bevier transformed her exclusive establishment into their private sanctuary.

"Those Fendi accessories would perfectly complement my new Mfume ensemble," Moni declared with the enthusiasm of someone discovering treasure, rushing toward the boutique before her friends could respond.

"We're already running behind schedule," Shaniece protested, checking her watch. "5:44, and for inferior designers like Fendi? Perhaps if it were Prada, but not this."

"Fashionably late has its own elegance," Coko countered, following Moni inside.

Samantha gestured toward the store entrance. "Should we join them?"

"I'd rather endure this cold than enter any establishment promoting Fendi's mediocrity," Shaniece replied with visible disdain. "Even their flagship locations lack authenticity."

"This competitive animosity toward Fendi needs resolution," Samantha observed, gently nudging her friend. "They didn't necessarily plagiarize your Montego Bay floating stage concept—brilliant ideas sometimes occur simultaneously to different minds."

"Someone leaked that information deliberately. They made me appear foolish, and I won't forget it."

While her friends browsed inside, Shaniece paced the sidewalk, wrestling with familiar restlessness. A couple passed by, their connection so genuine it stopped her mid-stride. The woman nestled securely against her partner's shoulder while his protective embrace conveyed devotion that transcended mere attraction. His eyes held eternal commitment—the kind of love Shaniece had once believed she'd found with Dalvin.

When did my marriage become so barren? The comparison stung deeply. For months, Dalvin's absences had grown longer, his explanations more elaborate, his deceptions increasingly transparent. What shocked her most was her growing indifference to his lies. Where once his betrayals had wounded her, now they merely confirmed what she'd already suspected.

Perhaps this emotional distance is protection, she mused. *The more he reveals his true character, the less power he holds over my heart.* In quiet moments, watching him sleep beside her, she sometimes felt like a poker player carefully concealing her hand while he unknowingly revealed his cards. *He believes he's deceiving me, but I'm the one with the winning strategy.*

Ché Pierre's Sanctuary

Upon arriving at the restaurant, Shaniece noted their tardiness with mild irritation. "I warned everyone we'd be late."

Her companions dismissed the grievance with practiced indifference, sweeping through the mahogany doors into an establishment that commanded reverence. The moment they crossed the threshold, Ché Pierre transformed them from mere patrons into guests of a bygone aristocracy.

Soaring ceilings adorned with hand-painted frescoes drew the eye upward, where cascading silk panels in deep burgundy and champagne created intimate alcoves within the grand space. Venetian crystal chandeliers—each a masterwork of cut glass and bronze—suspended like frozen fireworks, their multifaceted surfaces fracturing candlelight into dancing rainbows across the room.

The walls themselves seemed to breathe with history: ivory marble veined with gold leaf that caught and reflected the ambient glow, creating an almost ethereal luminescence. Antique mirrors in gilded frames multiplied the space infinitely, while Persian rugs in rich jewel tones cushioned their footsteps across polished marble floors.

The air carried whispers of bergamot and white tea, mingling with the subtle perfume of fresh orchids arranged in crystal vases throughout the space. Each table setting gleamed with sterling silver and bone China, positioned with mathematical precision that spoke to both artistry and devotion to craft.

As they moved deeper into this sanctuary of refinement, the very atmosphere seemed to elevate their bearing—shoulders straightened, voices softened, movements became more deliberate. Ché Pierre didn't merely serve dinner; it orchestrated an experience that transformed ordinary evenings into memories worthy of preservation.

"Renee' certainly understands the presentation and the assignment," Samantha murmured appreciatively.

"Indeed, she does," Shaniece agreed, feeling her earlier tensions begin to dissolve.

Their hostess appeared with characteristic warmth. "Ladies! Welcome to another evening of uninterrupted fellowship. I was beginning to wonder if I'd dine alone tonight."

"Traffic delays," Coko explained diplomatically while Shaniece prepared a more detailed excuse.

"Punctuality matters less than presence," Renee' declared graciously. "Please, make yourselves comfortable."

As they moved toward their private dining area, the group encountered Trange', a friend of Samantha's whose relationship with Shaniece remained perpetually strained. Two strong personalities in confined spaces often created predictable friction.

"Good evening, Trange'," Shaniece offered with practiced politeness that fooled no one.

"Likewise," Trange' responded with equal insincerity, her appraising look conveying mutual recognition of their territorial dynamics.

This woman tests my patience, Shaniece thought, but tonight belongs to our sisterhood, not petty rivalries.

The evening's harmony shattered when casual mention of their shopping excursion ignited a powder keg between Shaniece and Trange'. What began as offhand comments about design preferences quickly transformed into pointed barbs about artistic integrity versus commercial appeal.

Trange's eyes flashed with barely contained hostility as she questioned Shaniece's understanding of "authentic" fashion sensibilities. Shaniece, never one to retreat from intellectual combat, countered about market difficulty and consumer discernment. Their words became weapons—each carefully chosen syllable designed to wound pride and expose perceived inadequacies.

Just as the verbal duel threatened to escalate beyond civil discourse—with both women leaning forward like gladiators preparing for final combat—Moni's voice cut through the tension with masterful timing. She interrupted with urgent curiosity about recent developments in international affairs, her tone carrying just enough concern to make continued personal attacks seem petty and inappropriate.

The strategic intervention worked. Both combatants reluctantly disengaged, their pride still bristling but their public personas intact. The evening's peace hung by the thinnest of threads, restored but forever fragile.

Renee' escorted them to their reserved table, where tonight's curated selection represented the pinnacle of culinary artistry: herb-crusted prime rib aged twenty-eight days and slow-roasted to perfection, or wild-caught Atlantic salmon grilled over applewood and finished with a delicate citrus beurre blanc.

The entrées would be accompanied by truffle-infused fingerling potatoes, haricots verts almondine prepared with Madagascar vanilla, and locally sourced seasonal vegetables roasted in estate olive oil. Yet crowning this sophisticated feast—and perhaps most treasured of all—were her grandmother's legendary honey butter biscuits, their recipe unchanged for three generations, each one still hand-rolled with the same love and devotion that had graced family tables since childhood.

The familiar golden rounds served as both culinary anchor and emotional bridge, connecting the evening's refined elegance to cherished memories of simpler times, when love was measured not in exotic ingredients but in the warmth of hands that shaped dough with generational wisdom.

These humble biscuits, nestled among the evening's culinary sophistication, reminded each woman present that true nourishment comes not merely from what graces the plate, but from the sacred act of sharing sustenance with those who matter most.

"These biscuits transport me back to childhood," Samantha sighed contentedly. "Remember rushing to Mrs. Ida's house after cheerleading practice? Your grandmother was such a blessing to all of us."

The mention of Mrs. Ida Mae Lincoln transformed the atmosphere instantly. Even Trange' and Shaniece found their antagonism dissolving as memories of their beloved surrogate grandmother surfaced. Mrs. Ida had provided more than weekend childcare—she'd offered unconditional love, wisdom, and guidance that had shaped all their lives.

"I miss her terribly," Renee' whispered, tears beginning to flow. "She possessed such wisdom, always knowing exactly what we needed to hear. I used to resent her corrections, but she was invariably right." Her voice cracked as emotion overwhelmed carefully maintained composure.

Shaniece watched in amazement as her seemingly unshakeable friend crumbled before their eyes. Renee' had always embodied strength and control—seeing her vulnerable felt like witnessing Superman lose his powers. The mask of perfection had slipped, revealing raw humanity beneath polished success.

"Why didn't I listen to her guidance?" Renee' sobbed, striking the table with her fist.

Coko rushed to comfort her while Shaniece and Trange' exchanged glances of concern, their earlier conflict forgotten in face of their friend's obvious pain. Sometimes personal crisis creates unexpected unity among those who witness it.

"Marvin left me and our five children," Renee' announced through her tears, "for another man."

Silence crashed over the table like a physical force. Had they heard correctly? Dr. Marvin Jefferson—acclaimed psychiatrist, published author, the perfect husband everyone envied—living a secret life with a male lover?

"Are you certain?" Shaniece asked gently, though she dreaded the confirmation. Renee' and Marvin had represented her ideal of marital success, proof that true love could survive life's challenges.

"Absolutely certain," Renee' replied with bitter conviction.

"How did you discover this?" Coko inquired softly, bracing for painful details.

Renee's voice began as a whisper, each word clawing its way from depths she'd never intended to expose. "Eighteen months," she said, the numbers falling like stones into still water. "Eighteen months of watching the man I worshipped transform into a stranger."

Her hands trembled as she described the slow erosion of intimacy—how Marvin recoiled from her touch as though her skin burned him, how he began sculpting his body with obsessive care, how conversations died the moment she entered rooms where he spoke in hushed, urgent tones.

"I became a detective in my own home," she continued, her voice gaining dangerous momentum. "Analyzing receipts, memorizing his schedules, transforming into the very woman I'd once pitied—suspicious, desperate, pathetic."

The words came faster now, like blood from a reopened wound. She painted vivid scenes of rejected advances, of finding him meticulously grooming for mysterious appointments, of catching glimpses of text messages that vanished the instant she appeared.

"When I finally gathered courage to confront him—" Her voice cracked like breaking glass. "He backhanded me so hard I tasted copper for hours. Then he disappeared into the night, leaving me bleeding on our kitchen floor."

The table fell into cathedral silence, but Renee pressed forward with terrifying determination.

"His computer screen glowed like an accusation in our bedroom. Patient files, therapy notes, all mentioning this Staci—pages and pages documenting his 'journey of sexual discovery' with someone who ignited fires I apparently never could."

She laughed then—a sound devoid of humor, sharp enough to cut crystal.

"I armed myself like a warrior going to battle. Mace in one hand, my grandmother's carving knife in the other. I would confront this Staci, this woman who'd stolen my husband's heart, his body, his very soul."

Her eyes grew distant, seeing again that hotel room door.

"The sounds from inside—I knew them, recognized the rhythm of passion that had once belonged to me. I burst through expecting to find some temptress, some siren who'd bewitched my husband."

The pause stretched like a held breath before the storm breaks.

"Instead, I found my husband—the man who'd fathered my children, who'd sworn before God to honor me—on his knees before a boy barely old enough to vote. This golden-haired stranger who possessed everything I'd apparently failed to give."

Tears flowed freely now, but her voice never wavered.

"Time fractured. I became multiple women simultaneously—the wife, the mother, the betrayed woman, the potential murderer. The knife found its way to Marvin's throat before conscious thought could intervene. One motion, one simple slice, and my humiliation would end."

She touched her own throat, as if feeling phantom steel.

"In that moment, I glimpsed my true self—not the polished professional, not the devoted wife, not the nurturing mother, but something primal and terrifying. A woman who could kill without hesitation, who could watch blood pool and feel satisfaction rather than remorse."

The confession hung between them like a storm cloud.

"But divine intervention stayed my hand. Or perhaps simple cowardice. I'll never know which. I dropped that blade and walked away, leaving my marriage, my illusions, and perhaps my very identity scattered across that hotel room floor."

The silence that followed felt apocalyptic, as though the world itself had stopped spinning to absorb the magnitude of her revelation.

The Mask Removed

"I've spent years pretending," Renee' continued, her voice now steady with hard-won clarity. "Laughing at jokes that weren't funny, smiling when I wanted to cry, submitting when I knew he was wrong, maintaining appearances when everything was crumbling inside. That night, the woman behind the mask finally emerged—raw, furious, capable of violence I never imagined."

She looked around the table at her friends' faces. "It was terrifying but also liberating. No more pretending everything was perfect when it clearly wasn't. No more sacrificing my truth for his comfort."

Shaniece felt the words resonating deeply within her own experience. How many masks did she wear daily? How often did she smile while her heart broke, maintain composure while her world dissolved?

"The hardest part," Renee' concluded, "is realizing how much time I wasted trying to save something that was never real to begin with. Fifteen years of loving someone who was incapable of returning that love honestly."

Lord, grant us wisdom to see truth clearly, Shaniece prayed silently, and courage to remove our own masks when the time comes for authentic living.

The evening that had begun with superficial shopping discussions had transformed into something profound—a moment when one woman's courage to reveal her broken reality gave permission for others to examine their own carefully constructed façades.

Sometimes the greatest gift friends can offer each other is the safety to be authentically broken rather than artificially whole.

CHAPTER 5: THE DIVINE BALANCE

The Weight of Witness

Humid night air hung heavy throughout the bayou, an unusual oppression that seemed to mirror the spiritual atmosphere settling over Shaniece's life. Purple silk curtains stirred listlessly in the minimal breeze, carrying the faint scent of lilac—a fragrance that once brought comfort but now felt mocking in its sweetness.

Four months had passed since Renee's devastating revelation, four months of watching her dearest friend navigate the brutal dissolution of what everyone had believed was an ideal marriage. Standing beside Renee throughout the divorce proceedings had opened Shaniece's eyes to depths of human cruelty she'd never imagined possible. Marvin's public humiliation tactics, his vindictive courtroom revelations, his complete transformation from respected physician to vengeful adversary—it all served as a terrifying preface of what could happen when masks finally slipped away completely.

Supporting Renee meant choosing sides, and though it cost her a longstanding friendship with Marvin, Shaniece knew her loyalty belonged with the wounded rather than the one who inflicted wounds. Yet witnessing such systematic destruction of another woman's dignity left her questioning everything she thought she knew about marriage, commitment, and the men they'd trusted with their hearts.

During these same months, Dalvin's behavior had escalated beyond mere infidelity into something far more dangerous. The man who once wooed her with romantic picnics had become a stranger whose presence filled their home with tension and fear. Evidence of his betrayals no longer hid in shadows—hotel receipts, inappropriate photographs, and other signs of his double life appeared openly, as though he wanted her to discover them.

When she'd attempted to address these violations of their marriage covenant, his responses had grown increasingly aggressive. The final confrontation had crossed a line that changed everything between them—a moment when his hand raised against her revealed the true extent of his transformation. After that night, silence replaced communication, and Shaniece withdrew into herself, recognizing that the man she'd married no longer existed.

The Night That Shattered Everything

Sleep became an impossibility as restless energy coursed through her body, each toss and turn accompanied by glances at the merciless clock. 4:45 a.m. glowed accusingly in the darkness, marking another night of Dalvin's absence. His disappearances had evolved from occasional lapses into calculated abandonment, yet something sinister hung in the air tonight—an electrical charge that raised the hair on her arms and filled her spirit with inexplicable dread.

The oppressive heat drove her downstairs seeking refuge in ice water, hoping its coolness might calm both her fevered skin and anxious heart. But as she returned to their bedroom, her moment of private solitude shattered beneath the weight of an unwelcome presence.

Dalvin stood silhouetted in the doorway, his posture wrong somehow—swaying slightly, his usual controlled movements replaced by something predatory and unrecognizable. The acrid scent of alcohol mixed with something chemical filled the space between them, and his eyes held a wildness she'd never witnessed before.

What unfolded next would cleave her existence into distinct times: the woman she'd been before this moment, and the survivor she'd be forced to become. The violence that erupted transcended physical assault—though his fists and forced violations left their marks. This was spiritual warfare, an assault on her very soul orchestrated by someone who'd sworn before God to cherish and protect her.

Under the influence of substances that had stripped away his last vestiges of humanity, he crossed every sacred boundary with methodical cruelty. Her cries for mercy fell on ears deafened by artificial courage, her pleas for recognition meeting only the hollow stare of a stranger wearing her husband's face.

The bedroom that had once witnessed their love became a battlefield where innocence died and trust bled out across Egyptian cotton sheets. Every violation—physical, emotional, spiritual—carved deeper wounds than flesh could display. The man who'd promised to honor her before family and God revealed himself capable of horrors that would haunt her dreams for years to come.

When dawn's first light finally pierced through their curtains, it illuminated devastation beyond the physical damage etched across her bruised body. The sanctuary of their home had transformed into a chamber of trauma, every familiar surface now tainted with memories of betrayal so profound it challenged her faith in divine protection itself.

In those morning hours, as she surveyed the wreckage of everything she'd believed about love, marriage, and safety, one terrible truth crystallized: the greatest enemy she'd ever face lived under her own roof, sharing her name and wearing the face of her deepest trust.

Sunlight revealed truths that darkness had concealed. Lying broken on their bedroom floor, Shaniece faced the hardest question of her adult life: *How did I become this woman? How did I allow my life to reach this point?*

Fragments of memory surfaced—not just from the night's horrors, but from years of gradual erosion. She remembered being seventeen, pregnant, terrified, and making desperate choices that had cost her the ability to bear children. That trauma had bonded her to Dalvin through shared guilt and mutual dependence, creating a foundation built on fear rather than love.

Perhaps that's why I've tolerated so much, she realized with devastating clarity. I believed I deserved this treatment because of past mistakes.

Crawling to her vanity mirror, she studied her reflection—not only the physical evidence of violence, but the broken spirit behind her eyes. For too long, she'd worn masks of her own: the successful businesswoman, the devoted wife, the woman who had everything under control. Now, with those masks stripped away, she saw herself clearly for the first time in years.

"It's over," she whispered to her reflection. "This ends today."

The woman staring back at her bore little resemblance to the confident entrepreneur who commanded boardrooms and built business empires. But perhaps that was necessary. Perhaps she needed to be completely broken before she could be properly rebuilt.

God, I know I've made terrible choices. I know I've ignored Your warnings, Your gentle corrections, Your attempts to guide me toward something better. But I'm listening now. I'm ready to hear You now.

Standing slowly, each movement a testament to both physical pain and newfound resolve, Shaniece approached their dresser where she kept her grandmother's Bible—a gift she'd neglected for far too long. The pages fell open to Psalm 34: "The Lord is close to the brokenhearted and saves those who are crushed in spirit."

Crushed in spirit. The phrase resonated with surgical meticulousness. That's exactly what she was—crushed, broken, desperate for divine intervention.

But crushed things could be rebuilt. Broken vessels could be mended. Wounded spirits could be healed.

"Lord, I don't know how to do this," she prayed aloud, her voice steady despite her tears. "I don't know how to leave, where to go, or how to start over. But I know I can't stay here. I know this isn't Your plan for my life."

Her phone buzzed with a text from Samantha: "Haven't heard from you in days. Everything okay?"

For months, Shaniece had hidden the deterioration of her marriage behind carefully crafted responses and strategic absences. But sitting there with God's Word open before her and sunlight streaming through windows that had witnessed unspeakable darkness, she knew the time for pretense had ended.

She typed slowly: "I need help. Can you come over? Bring Renee if she's available. It's time to tell the truth."

The response came immediately: "On our way. Twenty minutes."

Twenty minutes to prepare for honesty. Twenty minutes to figure out how to explain the unexplainable.

Moving to her closet, she selected clothing that would conceal the worst evidence while allowing her to maintain some dignity.

But dignity, she realized, wasn't about hiding truth—it was about facing it with courage.

Father, give me strength for what comes next. Help me find the words. Help me trust the people You've placed in my life to love me through this.

As she prepared to open her life to scrutiny and support, Shaniece felt something she hadn't experienced in months: hope. Not hope that Dalvin would change—that illusion had died in the darkness. But hope that God could take even this catastrophic failure and transform it into something beautiful.

"And we know that in all things God works for the good of those who love him, who have been called according to his purpose."

She whispered the verse from Romans, clinging to its promise like a lifeline. Whatever came next, she wouldn't face it alone. She had sisters who would stand with her, a God who loved her unconditionally, and for the first time in years, the courage to choose truth over comfort.

The old Shaniece—the one who'd tolerated the intolerable, excused the inexcusable, and hidden behind masks of false contentment—that woman died in the darkness. The woman rising from the ashes would be different: scarred but not broken, wounded but not defeated, humbled but not destroyed.

This is where my real story begins, she thought, hearing Samantha's car in the driveway. *This is where I learn what it means to be truly free.*

CHAPTER 6: THE RECKONING

The phone's sharp ring pierced through Shaniece's solitude like a voice calling from another world. Two weeks had passed since that terrible night—two weeks of hiding behind drawn curtains and carefully constructed lies.

"Hello?" Her voice emerged hoarse, unused to conversation.

"Girl, you sound terrible. Where have you been? Are you alright?" Samantha's concern carried clearly through the phone as she navigated morning traffic toward her office.

"I'm recovering from this virus that's been...quite challenging," Shaniece replied, the half-truth sitting uncomfortably on her tongue. After her spiritual awakening, even small deceptions felt like betrayals of her newfound commitment to honesty.

Silence stretched between them—the kind pregnant with unspoken understanding.

"Shaniece." Samantha's voice had shifted, becoming the tone she used when confronting difficult truths. "I've been calling Dalvin for days. Your mother is worried sick. You've disappeared completely. This isn't about any virus."

The gentleness in her friend's voice nearly broke Shaniece's resolve to maintain privacy until she was stronger. But something in Samantha's inflection—a barely controlled anger—made her hesitate.

"Samantha, I need more time—"

"No." The word came with surprising force. "I'm hearing something in your voice that terrifies me. Whatever that man has done to you, we're going to handle it today."

Handle it. The phrase sent warning signals through Shaniece's spirit. She recognized that tone—the same dangerous edge she'd heard in Renee's voice when discussing her own desire for revenge against Marvin.

"What do you mean, 'handle it'?"

"Meet me at Amari's at two o'clock. If you don't show, I'm going to pay Dalvin a personal visit at his office, and I'm not going alone."

The Crossroads of Choice

After Samantha hung up, Shaniece sat in her living room holding the silent phone, wrestling with competing desires. Part of her—the wounded, angry part—wanted to unleash Samantha's protective fury on Dalvin. He deserved consequences for his actions. He deserved to face the pain he'd inflicted.

But another voice spoke more quietly in her spirit, reminding her of verses she'd been meditating on since her moment of surrender: *"Vengeance is mine, I will repay, says the Lord."*

The distinction between justice and vengeance had become crucial to her healing process. Justice sought restoration and protection for the innocent. Vengeance sought destruction and personal satisfaction. One honored God's character; the other elevated human emotion above divine wisdom.

Lord, help me want what You want, she prayed. Help me seek justice without becoming consumed by vengeance.

Rising slowly—her body still tender from trauma—she moved to the mirror that had become both enemy and teacher over the past weeks. The physical evidence of violence was fading, but the spiritual lessons remained vivid. She'd learned that God's justice operated on different principles than human revenge, and healing required surrendering her right to personal retaliation.

Sanctuary and Sisterhood

Amari's restaurant hummed with midday energy when Shaniece arrived, her carefully applied makeup concealing more than just physical bruises. She spotted Samantha immediately—her friend's entire frame coiled with barely contained fury.

"Thank the Lord," Samantha whispered, rising to envelop her in an embrace that conveyed both relief and protective rage. The hug stretched beyond normal bounds, and Shaniece felt her friend cataloging every subtle sign of healing, every remaining tender spot.

"Sit," Samantha commanded with tender authority. "It's time for the complete truth."

Shaniece drew a shuddering breath. Two weeks ago, she'd shared the surface wounds—Dalvin's infidelity, his increasing hostility, the slow death of their marriage. But today, with spiritual conviction weighing on her conscience, she knew half-truths served no one.

"Sam, what I told you before ... t wasn't everything." Her voice barely rose above a whisper. "That night—the night I disappeared—Dalvin came home intoxicated beyond recognition. Substances had transformed him into something demonic."

The words came in painful fragments: the violation that transcended physical assault, the spiritual warfare waged in their bedroom, the complete annihilation of every sacred boundary between husband and wife. She spoke of being reduced to prey in her own sanctuary, of experiencing evil wearing the face of promised love.

Samantha's complexion shifted through multiple shades of rage, her hands clenching and unclenching as though seeking something to destroy. "I want to call Pookie right now," she hissed. "I want that man erased from existence."

"I understand that fire," Shaniece replied, her voice gaining strength. "I've felt it consuming me from within. But these past weeks in prayer and study have shown me something crucial—God's justice operates on a different timeline than human vengeance."

"Don't you dare preach to me while that devil walks free," Samantha's voice cracked with anguish.

"I'm not advocating passivity. I'm discovering that divine justice penetrates deeper than any earthly retribution. What Dalvin did to me was evil, but if I respond with matching darkness, I become complicit in that same evil."

Shaniece pulled out her phone and opened her Bible app—a habit that had developed since her spiritual awakening. "Listen to this from Romans 12: 'Do not take revenge, my dear friends, but leave room for God's wrath, for it is written: It is mine to avenge; I will repay, says the Lord.'"

"That sounds like letting him get away with everything," Samantha protested.

"No, it sounds like trusting God to handle justice better than we can. But look at the next verses: 'If your enemy is hungry, feed him; if he is thirsty, give him something to drink. In doing this, you will heap burning coals on his head.' Do not be overcome by evil, but overcome evil with good.'"

Shaniece leaned forward. "The 'burning coals' aren't about torture—they're about conviction. When we respond to evil with righteousness, it exposes the darkness more powerfully than revenge ever could."

"So what does that look like practically?" Samantha asked, her anger beginning to mix with curiosity.

"It means I pursue legal justice through proper channels. I document everything, file police reports, seek restraining orders, pursue divorce proceedings with full disclosure of his behavior. I protect myself and potentially protect his future victims by creating legal consequences."

She paused, choosing her words carefully. "But I do it seeking his eventual restoration, not his destruction. I do it to stop the evil, not to satisfy my desire for revenge."

"That's incredibly difficult," Samantha admitted. "How do you separate justice from vengeance when you're the one who's been hurt?"

"Prayer. Community. Accountability. Recognizing that God's justice includes things I can't see or control." Shaniece's voice grew stronger. "Dalvin is destroying himself through his choices. His drug use, his violence, his sexual recklessness—these behaviors carry natural consequences that are already manifesting. My job isn't to accelerate his destruction; it's to protect myself and others while praying for his eventual repentance."

"And if he never repents?"

"Then God's justice will be perfect, even if I don't see it in this lifetime. But if I pursue vengeance instead of justice, I become corrupted by the same evil that hurt me."

Samantha sat back, processing this perspective. "So what do you need from me?"

"Help me find a good attorney. Support me through the legal process. Pray with me when I'm tempted toward bitterness. And help me remember that healing doesn't require his destruction—it requires my obedience to God's way of handling injustice."

Over the following weeks, Shaniece implemented her plan with careful attention to biblical principles. She filed police reports, not from vengeance but from responsibility to protect other potential victims. She documented Dalvin's behavior, not to embarrass him publicly but to establish legal grounds for divorce and personal protection.

She consulted with Christian counselors who helped her process trauma while maintaining spiritual health. She surrounded herself with believers who could pray for both her healing and Dalvin's eventual restoration.

Most challenging of all, she began praying for Dalvin's deliverance from the demons that had consumed him—not because she wanted to reconcile, but because she wanted him to find the freedom that comes only through genuine repentance.

"Lord," she prayed one evening as sunset painted her living room in gentle light, "I give You my desire for revenge. I give You my anger, my hurt, my demand that he pay for what he's done. I trust Your justice to be more complete and more healing than anything I could devise. Help me overcome evil with good."

As weeks passed, she watched divine justice unfold in ways her human mind couldn't have orchestrated. Dalvin's drug use led to consequences at work. His reckless behavior resulted in legal complications. His violence created enemies in unexpected places.

But rather than taking satisfaction in his downfall, Shaniece found herself praying more earnestly for his salvation. She had learned that true victory over evil doesn't come through destroying one's enemies—it comes through loving them enough to want their redemption while protecting oneself from their harmful choices.

This is what it means to be more than a conqueror, she realized. Not conquering through revenge, but conquering through love, justice, and trust in God's perfect timing.

CHAPTER 7: THE ULTIMATE TEST

The Sword Falls

Thunder carved jagged paths across Lake Pontchartrain's darkening waters as Margaux Morrison's Mercedes cut through rain-slicked streets toward One Canal Place. The storm's intensity seemed to mirror the spiritual warfare Shaniece had been waging in prayer these past weeks—violent, cleansing, inevitable.

Inside the vehicle's cocoon of Italian leather, Shaniece held a manila envelope containing documents she'd already signed in Margaux's office that morning—divorce filings, restraining orders, asset protection motions. These papers represented her written declaration that God's people need not remain victims of evil masquerading as marriage.

"The papers are filed and processed," Margaux confirmed, checking her watch as they approached the legal district. "In exactly forty-three minutes, at 3:17 PM, sheriff's deputies will serve Dalvin during his weekly staff meeting. Maximum witnesses, minimum opportunity for damage control."

Shaniece watched raindrops streak the passenger window like tears she'd shed in countless midnight hours of prayer. "He'll claim this is evidence of my instability."

"Then we'll allow his response to reveal his character. Genuine repentance manifests very differently than strategic reputation management."

But something crucial remained unspoken—Margaux's briefcase contained a sealed investigator's report documenting Dalvin's activities with photographic accuracy. Evidence that would surface when needed most.

Meanwhile, across the city, the elevator climbed as Deputy Marshal James Crawford studied his service instructions. High-profile case involving prominent business figures—discretional handling required written in bold red like blood on the envelope.

The reception area was crowded as Crawford approached the polished desk.

"Ma'am, I need to speak with Dalvin Shaw regarding urgent legal matters."

Dalvin's corner office buzzed with pre-weekend energy as his marketing team gathered around presentation boards. Through floor-to-ceiling windows, he orchestrated their Friday planning session with characteristic commanding presence, unaware that his carefully constructed world was about to implode.

"Mr. Shaw?" Crawford's voice sliced through corporate chatter with judicial authority. "You've been served with court documents requiring immediate attention."

The room fell silent. Papers rustled with the whisper of reputation disintegrating. Dalvin's face cycled through confusion, recognition, and pure rage as he scanned the documents.

"Everyone out. NOW!" His voice carried dangerous undertones that scattered employees like startled birds.

Alone with legal documents that spelled out his wife's accusations in clinical detail, Dalvin Shaw began calculating his counter-attack.

When Foundations Crack

FaLessia's fingers trembled as she held the phone, watching rain streak her office windows while her worldview collapsed in real time. The court documents lay scattered across her desk like evidence of some cosmic mistake—domestic violence, substance abuse, adultery. Words that couldn't possibly describe the brother who'd walked her down the aisle when their father was deployed overseas.

"Mama, please tell me you haven't seen the news yet."

Silence stretched across the phone line, heavy with unspoken knowledge.

"Child, I've been expecting this call for months." Their mother's voice carried decades of watching her son destroy himself. "The only surprise is that it took this long."

"How can you say that?" FaLessia's carefully controlled composure cracked. "This is Dalvin we're talking about. Your son. My brother. The man who paid for my education, who walked me down the aisle—"

"The same man who came to Sunday dinner reeking of alcohol and strange perfume. The same man whose eyes went cold when he looked at his wife. The same man who stopped calling unless he needed something."

FaLessia sank into her chair as if physical weight was pressing down on her chest. Through her window, she could see the homeless shelter where she'd spent countless hours serving meals and offering hope to broken people. How had she missed her own brother's brokenness?

"I have to choose between them, don't I?" The words escaped as barely a whisper.

"No, baby. You have to choose between truth and comfortable lies. Between enabling destruction and supporting healing. That's not really a choice at all."

Rain drummed against glass like accusations demanding acknowledgment. In the distance, lightning illuminated the city where her brother's reputation was burning to ash while her sister-in-law fought for her very life.

"What if I've been wrong about everything?"

"Then you get to start fresh with truth as your foundation. That's not a curse, FaLessia. That's grace."

Shaniece's office felt like a stage set for confrontation when security announced Dalvin's arrival. The mahogany desk became a barrier, floor-to-ceiling windows transformed into backdrops, and leather chairs positioned like props for the most important performance of their marriage.

He entered carrying flowers—white roses that mocked the innocence they'd lost years ago. His clothes were immaculate, his expression crafted to project vulnerability and remorse. The man was a masterpiece of calculated emotion.

"Baby." The word dripped with rehearsed pain. "I just left my lawyer's office. Please tell me this is some kind of nightmare I'll wake up from."

Shaniece remained seated, creating psychological distance that physical space couldn't provide. "The only nightmare, Dalvin, is the one I've been living. This is the moment I finally wake up."

He collapsed into the chair across from her desk with theatrical precision—shoulders slumped, head in hands, the perfect picture of a broken man seeking redemption. If she hadn't lived through months of his escalating violence, the performance might have been convincing.

"I know I've made terrible mistakes." Tears appeared on cue, glistening under office lighting. "But God is working on my heart, baby. I feel Him convicting me of my sins. We can fix this. Counseling, rehab, whatever it takes. I'll do anything to save our marriage."

His voice cracked at precisely the right moment. His hands reached toward her with practiced desperation. Every gesture calculated to trigger her protective instincts and override her rational judgment.

"Dalvin." Her voice remained steady as an anchor during a storm. "If God is truly working in your heart, that work will continue regardless of my response. Genuine repentance doesn't require an audience to sustain it."

The mask slipped for just a moment—eyes flashing with anger before vulnerability returned. "You're not even willing to try? Fifteen years mean nothing to you?"

"Fifteen years mean everything to me. That's precisely why I won't allow you to destroy them completely by enabling your continued self-destruction."

She rose from her chair, moving to the windows where city lights twinkled below like stars in a universe that kept spinning despite personal catastrophes. "Your relationship with God shouldn't depend on my willingness to remain in danger. If you truly want healing, pursue it for its own sake."

"So that's it?" The façade cracked wider, revealing the rage beneath. "You're just giving up on us?"

"I'm giving up on pretending that love means accepting abuse. I'm giving up on believing that my patience can save someone who doesn't want salvation. I'm choosing truth over comfortable lies."

Thunder crashed overhead as if Heaven itself was punctuating her declaration. When she turned from the window, Dalvin was gone—leaving only wilted roses and the lingering scent of cologne that once made her heart race and now made her stomach turn.

Circling Vultures

Dawn broke gray and ominous over the French Quarter as Hermosa's stock price flickered across financial news feeds like a weakened heartbeat. By 7 AM, Shaniece's phone buzzed with predatory sympathy disguised as business concern.

Marcus Fitzgerald's voice oozed false compassion through her Bluetooth speaker as she navigated morning traffic. "Darling, I'm simply heartbroken about your personal situation. These tabloid vultures must be making everything so much more difficult."

His concern was as authentic as a three-dollar bill, but Shaniece had been expecting this call since the divorce papers became public record.

"The media attention is manageable, Marcus. Hermosa's fundamentals remain strong regardless of personal circumstances."

"Of course, of course. But market perception can be so … unforgiving. If you're looking to reduce stress during this difficult transition, I'd be honored to discuss taking this burden off your shoulders. A fair acquisition that would allow you to focus on healing."

She pulled into Hermosa's executive parking garage, noting the cluster of reporters already gathering near the building's entrance. Sharks smelling blood in corporate waters.

"How thoughtful of you to call so early with such a generous offer," she replied, her voice carrying enough ice to freeze the Mississippi. "But I'm afraid you've misunderstood the situation entirely. Personal challenges don't weaken me, Marcus—they refine me. And Hermosa has never been stronger."

"Well, certainly, but the market uncertainty—"

"Will stabilize once investors realize that my company was built on vision and execution, not marital status. But thank you for your concern. I'm sure you'll find other opportunities that align better with your...acquisition strategy."

She ended the call and sat in her car for a moment, watching rain begin to fall on the garage's concrete floors. Three more similar calls would come before noon. By tomorrow, at least five competitors would have approached board members with whispered concerns about leadership stability.

Let them come, she thought, gathering her briefcase and steeling herself for battle. They're about to learn why I built an empire in the first place.

War Council

The Hermosa boardroom pulsed with electric tension when Shaniece swept through its mahogany doors at precisely 9 AM. Twelve faces arranged around the polished conference table—some radiating loyalty, others calculating weakness, all hungry to witness whether their CEO would collapse under scandal's weight or rise like a phoenix from personal ashes.

She had chosen her battle attire deliberately: a midnight black Yves Saint Laurent power suit that sculpted her frame like liquid authority, paired with crimson Louboutin heels that clicked against marble floors with the rhythm of approaching conquest. Diamond studs caught the morning light filtering through storm clouds, while her hair, swept into a severe chignon, transformed her into something between corporate warrior and avenging angel.

"Ladies and gentlemen." Her voice sliced through ambient tension with judicial precision. "I assume your morning caffeine consumption included sufficient tabloid material regarding my private affairs. Rather than permit speculation to metastasize like cancer through our organization, I will provide clarification only once."

Thunder rolled across Lake Pontchartrain as lightning illuminated the storm brewing beyond floor-to-ceiling windows. Nature itself seemed choreographed to underscore the drama unfolding thirty floors above New Orleans' financial district.

"I'm divorcing my husband because his behavior has become incompatible with my values and what this company stands for. This wasn't an easy decision, especially knowing it would create...complications for Hermosa."

She moved with predatory grace toward the head of the table, where architectural models of their Chicago expansion gleamed under recessed lighting—three-dimensional proof of vision transforming into profitable reality.

"However, my personal relationships have never powered Hermosa's ascension to greatness, nor will they orchestrate our descent. Our quarterly returns speak with greater authority than gossip columns ever could. Our expansion schedule advances without modification. Our commitment to excellence burns with increased intensity."

Board member Patricia Chen shifted forward, her expression blending genuine concern with opportunistic calculation. "What about media attention? How do we navigate public relations while this...situation evolves?"

"Through transparency regarding business operations and strategic silence concerning private matters. We will neither retreat from scrutiny nor permit it to divert us from revolutionizing global fashion markets."

"And if your husband attempts to claim business assets or disrupts operations?"

Shaniece's smile could have shattered reinforced glass. "Dalvin Shaw possesses zero legal standing regarding Hermosa. This empire preceded our union and will dominate international markets long after our divorce finalizes. Any interference attempts will trigger overwhelming legal warfare and complete corporate annihilation."

Silence descended except for rain drumming window glass and the soft whisper of climate control. She had alchemized potential catastrophe into opportunity, vulnerability into strength, personal devastation into professional battle cry.

"Furthermore," she continued, her voice gathering force like approaching hurricane winds, "any board member questioning my leadership during this transition may liquidate their shares immediately. I constructed this empire from nothing once. Reconstruction would merely provide entertainment."

The session concluded with renewed confidence radiating from allies and visible anxiety flickering across potential deserters' faces. As board members departed, several lingered to offer private support, while others initiated hushed phone conversations that would reach competitors before lunch ended.

Alone in her office as sunset painted New Orleans in shades of amber and rose, Shaniece stood before windows that had witnessed the day's battles. Below, traffic moved through streets where her personal drama was becoming public entertainment, where competitors circled like sharks, where family members chose sides in a war she never wanted to fight.

Her phone displayed dozens of missed calls—reporters seeking statements, business associates offering hollow sympathy, and society friends whose loyalty evaporated when tested by scandal. But three messages rose above the noise:

Samantha: "Watched your press conference online. You handled those vultures like the queen you are. Proud to stand with you."

Renee: "Courage is contagious, sister. Your strength gives me strength."

Her mother: "Sometimes the hardest battles produce the strongest warriors. You were magnificent today. Love you, baby girl."

Opening her Bible app to familiar comfort, she found Psalm 35 glowing on her screen: "Vindicate me, my God, and plead my cause against an unfaithful nation. Rescue me from those who are deceitful and wicked."

Lord, I see Your hand orchestrating all of this. You're protecting me through legal systems I never understood, giving me wisdom to discern manipulation from genuine remorse, surrounding me with people who value truth over convenience.

Lightning illuminated the city below as thunder rolled across the river like divine applause. The reckoning had begun, but she no longer faced it alone. God's justice was unfolding with perfect timing and overwhelming power.

Her reflection in the darkened window showed a woman transformed—scarred but not broken, wounded but not defeated, refined by fire and strengthened by truth. The old Shaniece might have been destroyed by this level of public scrutiny and personal betrayal.

However, the woman emerging from this crucible was being forged for purposes she couldn't yet comprehend, prepared for battles she had yet to imagine, equipped with weapons that would reshape not only her own destiny, but the lives of countless others who needed to witness authentic courage in action.

Let the war continue, she thought, watching storm clouds retreat toward the Gulf. *I know Who fights beside me.*

CHAPTER 8: WHEN SISTERHOOD FRACTURES

S haniece's phone erupted at 5:47 AM with the kind of call that shatters executive dreams into corporate nightmares. David Chen, Hermosa's Chief Financial Officer, sounded like a man delivering news of sudden death.

"You need to get to the office immediately. We have a catastrophic situation."

Twenty minutes later, she stood in the emergency boardroom where David's laptop displayed financial devastation across multiple screens. Numbers that made no sense. Accounts that should have contained millions now showed critical shortfalls. Credit lines mysteriously frozen. Investment portfolios liquidated without authorization.

"How is this possible?" Her voice remained steady despite the chaos spiraling through her mind.

"Joint accounts. Investment partnerships established during your marriage. Dalvin had access to more assets than we realized." David's fingers flew across his keyboard, revealing the scope of financial sabotage. "He's been systematically draining resources for months, using legal loopholes we never anticipated."

The conference room's floor-to-ceiling windows revealed dawn breaking over a city where her empire was crumbling in real time. Hermosa's stock price plummeted as word spread through financial networks faster than wildfire through drought-stricken forests.

"How long do we have?"

"Without immediate capital infusion? Six weeks. Maybe eight if we suspend the Chicago expansion and lay off three hundred employees."

Margaux Morrison's emergency call came at 7:15 AM, her attorney's voice carrying grim satisfaction mixed with professional concern. "I've reviewed the financial documents. Technically, everything he's done was legal. Joint accounts, shared investments, partnerships established before separation papers were filed. He played a very long game, Shaniece."

"So I have no recourse?"

"Civil litigation could take years. Criminal charges would require proving intent to defraud, which becomes complicated in marital dissolution cases. He's covered his tracks well."

Shaniece's phone buzzed with her mother's contact photo as she sat alone in her office, staring at bankruptcy projections that mocked fifteen years of tireless building. She almost ignored the call—until something in her spirit whispered urgency.

"Baby girl, I'm at Ochsner Medical Center. I need you to come now."

The drive through morning traffic blurred past like a fever dream. Her mother's voice had carried something beyond normal concern—a trembling that spoke of genuine medical crisis rather than routine doctor visits.

Room 314 contained the woman who had been Shaniece's rock through every childhood storm, now looking fragile and diminished against stark white sheets. Machines beeped with electronic rhythm while IV tubes snaked toward hands that had once seemed invincible.

"Mama, what happened?"

"Heart attack. Small one, they say, but enough to remind me that time isn't unlimited." Her mother's eyes held clarity despite the medical equipment surrounding her. "Sit down, child. We need to talk about forgiveness."

The word landed like a physical blow. "Mama, if this is about Dalvin—"

"This is about your soul, not your marriage. I've been thinking about what forgiveness means when someone has truly hurt you. Whether mercy requires reconciliation or just releasing poison from your own heart."

"The doctors said you shouldn't be stressed—"

"Child, I've been stressed watching my daughter carry hatred that's eating her alive. That's more dangerous than any heart condition."

Through the hospital window, Shaniece could see Lake Pontchartrain stretching toward horizons where her business empire was dissolving and her future seemed increasingly uncertain. Now her mother—her last source of unconditional support—was challenging the very foundation of her healing process.

"He destroyed everything I built, Mama. He nearly destroyed me."

"And if you let bitterness consume you, he'll complete the job from a distance. Forgiveness isn't about him, baby. It's about freeing yourself to become who God created you to be."

Samantha appeared in the hospital corridor like an avenging angel, her heels clicking against polished floors with purpose that could be heard three rooms away. Under her arm, she carried a manila envelope that seemed to pulse with dangerous energy.

"We need to talk. Privately. Now."

They found refuge in the hospital chapel—a small interfaith sanctuary where stained glass windows cast rainbow patterns across simple wooden pews. The irony wasn't lost on Shaniece that divine guidance was about to be tested in the literal presence of sacred space.

"Pookie came through with information that changes everything." Samantha's voice carried satisfaction mixed with something darker. "Dalvin's been sloppy. Financial records, drug transactions, evidence of multiple affairs including with married women whose husbands have influence. We can destroy him completely."

The envelope contained photographs, bank statements, text message transcripts, and medical records obtained through methods Shaniece preferred not to examine too closely. Each document represented ammunition powerful enough to obliterate not just Dalvin's reputation but his entire future.

"This could expose his drug suppliers, his affair partners, his financial crimes. He'd face criminal charges, professional censure, social destruction. Complete annihilation."

Shaniece studied evidence that could solve all her problems. Dalvin's law firm would drop him immediately. His family would disown him. Criminal prosecution would follow. The man who had systematically destroyed her life could be utterly ruined within days.

"There's more." Samantha's voice dropped to a whisper despite their solitude. "One of his affair partners is a judge's wife. Another is a city councilman's daughter. This doesn't just destroy Dalvin—it takes down powerful people who've been protecting him."

The weight of potential vengeance felt simultaneously liberating and nauseating. Justice served with overwhelming force. Complete vindication. Total victory.

"What do you need me to do?"

"Nothing. Just give me permission to release this information to the right journalists, the right prosecutors, the right people who can ensure he pays for everything he's done to you."

The Divine Wrestling Match

That evening, alone in her mother's hospital room while medical staff conducted shift changes, Shaniece spread the evidence across a bedside table like tarot cards revealing futures she could choose. Her mother slept fitfully, connected to machines that measured heartbeats and oxygen levels while her daughter wrestled with questions that would define her character for years to come.

Her phone buzzed with messages from board members demanding action, creditors seeking payment schedules, and employees worried about job security. Hermosa was hemorrhaging reputation and resources while her personal life provided tabloid entertainment for a city that loved watching powerful women fall from grace.

Using this evidence would solve everything. Dalvin's destruction would restore her credibility, provide legal leverage for asset recovery, and satisfy everyone demanding justice. The Christian community that had watched her suffer would applaud his downfall. Her business associates would respect her willingness to fight with every available weapon.

But in the chapel's stained-glass light, she had remembered Jesus on the cross—having the power to destroy his accusers but choosing a different path entirely. Divine strength expressed through restraint rather than retaliation.

"Father, forgive them, for they know not what they do."

The verse echoed through her mind as she studied photographs that could end Dalvin's life as he knew it. Was this justice or vengeance? Was she being called to mercy or simply being manipulated by religious concepts that protected abusers?

Her Bible app glowed with familiar comfort: "Beloved, never avenge yourselves, but leave it to the wrath of God, for it is written, 'Vengeance is mine, I will repay, says the Lord.'"

But Romans 13 also spoke of governmental authority as God's instrument for justice: "For he is God's servant for your good. But if you do wrong, be afraid, for he does not bear the sword in vain."

The evidence before her could serve justice through proper legal channels. But it could also satisfy her desire for revenge through public humiliation and complete destruction.

By morning, word of the evidence had somehow leaked through networks of protective friends who believed Shaniece deserved overwhelming vindication. Her phone rang constantly with supporters urging decisive action.

Renee called from her own divorce attorney's office: "Girl, use everything you have. Show them what happens when they mess with strong women. Make an example of him."

Business associates offered resources to ensure maximum media coverage. Church members whispered about divine justice requiring human action. Even her personal assistant suggested that mercy toward Dalvin would be interpreted as weakness by competitors circling Hermosa like vultures.

The pressure felt suffocating—everyone expecting her to unleash destruction while her spirit whispered about a narrow path that led through forgiveness rather than revenge.

Margaux Morrison's call came at noon with updates that made the decision even more crucial: "Dalvin's legal team knows you have damaging information. They're preparing preemptive character assassination, claiming you've fabricated evidence out of vindictiveness. If you're going to use what you have, it needs to happen in the next forty-eight hours."

Standing in the hospital corridor where her mother fought for physical healing while her daughter battled for spiritual survival, Shaniece faced the ultimate test of everything she claimed to believe about faith, forgiveness, and divine justice.

Lord, show me the difference between being your instrument of justice and being consumed by my own desire for revenge. Help me choose the path that honors You, even if it costs me everything I've worked to build.

Through the window, storm clouds gathered over Lake Pontchartrain while her phone buzzed with another message from Samantha: "Clock's ticking. Do we destroy him or let him destroy you? Your choice."

The envelope of evidence seemed to burn against her fingers as she realized that her response to this moment would determine not just her future, but the woman she would become in the aftermath of ultimate betrayal.

CHAPTER 9: DIVINE INTERVENTION

____

The Emergency Summit

The private dining room at Commander's Palace felt like a war council chamber when Shaniece arrived at precisely noon. Samantha had orchestrated this emergency gathering with unwavering focus—Renee, Moni, Coko, and even Trange' assembled around a mahogany table that reflected the crystal chandelier light like a mirror pool. The absence of their usual laughter created an atmosphere thick with tension and unspoken agendas.

"Thank you all for coming on such short notice," Samantha began, her executive bearing transforming lunch into a board meeting. "We're here because our sister is facing the fight of her life, and I need to know who's truly with her."

Shaniece felt exposed under their collective gaze—five women who had shared secrets, dreams, and years of unconditional support now studying her like a puzzle they couldn't quite solve. The manila envelope containing Dalvin's destruction sat beside Samantha's water glass like a loaded weapon waiting for deployment.

"Girl, we've all seen the financial news," Moni declared, her usual playfulness replaced by business-minded concern. "Hermosa's stock is in free fall. The blogs are saying you're finished. What's the tea?"

"Dalvin systematically drained joint accounts and investments," Shaniece replied, her voice steady despite the magnitude of admission. "We're facing potential bankruptcy unless I find immediate capital or..." She gestured toward the envelope. "Unless I use what Samantha discovered to destroy him completely."

Renee leaned forward, her own divorce battle having sharpened her instincts for warfare. "What exactly are we talking about? How devastating is this evidence?"

Samantha's smile carried predatory satisfaction. "Devastating enough to end his career, his reputation, and his freedom. Drug transactions, financial crimes, affairs with powerful men's wives. We're talking complete annihilation."

"Then what's the problem?" Trange' demanded, her voice cutting through diplomatic politeness. "Use it. Destroy him. Show every man in New Orleans what happens when they try to break strong women."

The Moral Divide

The room erupted in overlapping conversations as each woman processed the implications differently. Coko's quiet voice eventually rose above the chaos: "Wait. Are we seriously discussing whether to show mercy to someone who nearly destroyed Shaniece?"

"I'm discussing whether to become the kind of person who chooses revenge over righteousness," Shaniece replied, her words creating immediate silence. "Using this evidence would violate everything I claim to believe about forgiveness and divine justice."

Moni's expression shifted from confusion to concern. "Baby girl, forgiveness doesn't mean letting someone completely ruin your life without consequences. That's not biblical—that's foolish."

"There's a difference between legal consequences and personal destruction," Shaniece countered. "I can pursue divorce, asset recovery, and protection through proper channels without releasing information designed to humiliate and destroy."

Renee's laugh carried bitter edges. "Honey, I tried taking the high road with Marvin. You know what that got me? Public humiliation while he walked away with half our assets and his reputation intact. Sometimes the high road leads straight off a cliff."

The philosophical divide crystallized around the table like battle lines being drawn. Samantha, Renee, and Trange' formed a coalition advocating total warfare, while Coko and Moni wrestled with competing loyalties between friendship and principles.

"Let me understand this correctly," Trange' said, her voice dripping with incredulity. "You have the power to end this man who abused you, who's trying to destroy your business, who's shown you no mercy whatsoever—and you're considering showing him mercy because of religious principles?"

"I'm considering it because revenge transforms victims into villains. Because choosing God's way over my way requires trusting that His justice is more complete than anything I can orchestrate."

Samantha stood abruptly, her chair scraping against hardwood floors with the sound of frustration finding physical expression. The movement commanded attention and revealed the depth of her concern for a sister she couldn't bear to watch self-destruct.

"Shaniece, you know I love you more than my own blood family. We've been through everything together—childhood, business building, heartbreak, triumph." Her voice carried the raw emotion of someone watching a loved one make choices that seemed self-destructive. "But I'm watching you sacrifice everything real and tangible for something ... don't understand."

She moved to the window overlooking the Garden District, her reflection ghostlike against Spanish moss that draped ancient oaks. "I've fought beside you for years. I've celebrated your victories and held you through defeats. I've seen you transform from that scared pregnant teenager into the most powerful businesswoman in Louisiana."

Turning back to face her dearest friend, Samantha's eyes glistened with unshed tears. "And now I'm supposed to watch you lose everything because you believe showing mercy to a man who tried to destroy you is somehow the right thing to do?"

"Sam, I know this is hard to understand—"

"It is hard to understand!" The words erupted with sisterly desperation. "I see you choosing principles over protection, faith over fighting back, and I'm terrified of what that's going to cost you. Not just financially—emotionally, spiritually, everything."

Her voice broke slightly as the weight of loyal concern overwhelmed executive composure. "What if your mercy enables him to hurt someone else? What if your forgiveness sends a message that successful women can be broken without consequences? What if I must watch my sister lose everything because she's too good for this cruel world?"

Samantha reached for the envelope, her hands trembling with emotion rather than anger. "I can't force you to save yourself. But I can't stand by and watch you choose destruction either. If you won't protect yourself, then I have to try to protect you."

"Samantha, please." Shaniece's voice carried both authority and pleading. "That's not your burden to carry."

"You became my burden to carry the day we became sisters. That doesn't change because we disagree about how to handle this situation."

Moni's attempted mediation fell flat against the intensity of emotion charging the atmosphere. "Can't we find some middle ground? Use some of the evidence but not all of it? Enough to protect Shaniece without completely destroying him?"

"Partial destruction is still destruction," Shaniece replied. "Either I trust God's justice or I don't. Either I believe forgiveness has power or I don't. There's no comfortable compromise between those positions."

Coko's quiet wisdom cut through the debate: "What if God's justice includes using the evidence? What if refusing to act is actually enabling Dalvin to hurt other women?"

The question hung in the air like incense, heavy with implications none of them wanted to fully examine. Shaniece felt the foundations of her spiritual certainty shifting beneath philosophical pressure from people she trusted most.

Trange' seized the moment of doubt: "Exactly. You're not protecting Dalvin—you're *failing* to protect his future victims. That's not righteousness, that's cowardice disguised as virtue."

"And what about us?" Renee added, her voice carrying hurt that ran deeper than tactical disagreement. "We've stood by you through everything. Supported you, defended you, sacrificed for you. Now you're choosing abstract principles over concrete loyalty to the women who've actually been there."

The accusation cut deepest because it contained truth. These women had indeed sacrificed for their friendship—time, resources, emotional energy, professional relationships. They had earned the right to expect her trust and cooperation.

"I'm not choosing principles over friendship," Shaniece protested. "I'm trying to make the choice that honors both without compromising either."

"Then you're failing at both," Samantha declared with finality that felt like a door slamming shut. "Because friendship requires trust, and you clearly don't trust us to understand what's best for your situation."

The confrontation escalated when Renee stood to join Samantha, their alliance creating visible division around the table. "I went through my divorce trying to maintain dignity while Marvin destroyed me piece by piece. I will not watch another sister make the same mistake."

"This is different—"

"No, it's not!" Renee's composure shattered completely. "It's exactly the same pattern. Abusive man systematically destroys woman. Woman has opportunity to fight back. Woman chooses 'forgiveness' over protection. Woman loses everything while abuser faces no consequences."

Moni and Coko exchanged glances that spoke of friendships being tested beyond their breaking points. The sisterhood that had sustained them through decades was fracturing along lines they had never imagined possible.

"Maybe we should take a break," Coko suggested desperately. "Let emotions cool down, think about this more carefully—"

"There's no time for cooling down," Samantha interrupted. "Each day Shaniece delays gives Dalvin more opportunity to destroy what's left of her empire. Every day she hesitates sends a message to every predator in New Orleans that successful women can be broken without consequences."

She gathered her purse with movements that communicated finality. "I've done everything I can to support you, Shaniece. But I won't stand by and watch you commit financial and professional suicide because you've confused weakness with virtue."

"If you walk out that door with that envelope—"

"You'll what? Forgive me too?" Samantha's laugh carried no humor whatsoever. "At some point, unlimited forgiveness becomes unlimited enablement. At some point, mercy without justice becomes injustice itself."

The other women watched in horrified silence as their closest friendship disintegrated before their eyes. Years of shared secrets, mutual support, and unconditional loyalty were dissolving in philosophical acid none of them knew how to neutralize.

"Choose," Samantha demanded, her hand on the envelope that contained the power to save or damn everything Shaniece had worked to build. "Your principles or your future. Your theology or your reality."

The Aftermath

As Samantha walked out of Commander's Palace with Dalvin's secrets clutched in her manicured fingers, the remaining women sat in stunned silence. The elegant dining room that had hosted countless celebrations now felt like a funeral parlor where their sisterhood lay in state.

"She's not wrong about everything," Moni whispered, her voice barely audible above the restaurant's ambient noise. "The practical concerns are real. The consequences are devastating."

"But so is the spiritual crisis," Coko replied. "If Shaniece compromises her convictions under pressure, what does that say about the faith that's supposed to sustain her through trials?"

Trange' gathered her belongings with visible disgust. "I can't respect someone who chooses abstract ideals over concrete loyalty. Samantha's right—this isn't virtue, it's cowardice."

As her friends departed one by one—some in anger, others in confusion, all in disappointment—Shaniece remained alone at a table set for six. The silence felt deafening after hours of passionate debate about the nature of justice, mercy, and friendship.

Her phone buzzed with a text from Samantha: "I'm sorry it came to this. But I won't watch you destroy yourself. The information goes public in 24 hours unless you stop me."

Lord, she prayed in the emptiness of abandoned fellowship, I thought choosing Your way would bring peace, not isolation. I thought doing right would strengthen relationships, not destroy them. Help me understand why standing for truth feels so much like standing alone.

Through the restaurant's historic windows, storm clouds gathered over the Garden District like divine commentary on human relationships tested beyond their capacity to endure. The choice between friendship and faith had become the choice between everything she'd built and everything she believed.

She still had twenty-four hours to decide which sacrifice her soul could actually survive.

CHAPTER 10: THE DIVINE PAYBACK

***

The Weight of Betrayal

The wrought iron gates of Samantha's Garden District mansion closed behind her Mercedes with mechanical finality, sealing her inside a fortress of regret and marble columns. Spanish moss draped the centuries-old live oaks like funeral shrouds, their branches reaching toward her antebellum home as if nature itself was pleading for wisdom she wasn't sure she possessed.

She sat in her circular driveway for twenty minutes, engine cooling while her conscience burned. The manila envelope lay beside her on Italian leather seats like a loaded weapon she wasn't certain she had the right to fire. Through her windshield, the Greek Revival mansion her great-great-grandfather had built rose three stories into storm clouds that matched her internal weather perfectly.

What have I done?

The question echoed through chambers of her heart where loyalty to Shaniece had always resided without question or compromise. For fifteen years, they'd been more than friends—they'd been chosen sisters who'd navigated every crisis together, who'd built empires side by side, who'd sworn nothing would ever divide them.

Now she'd walked out on her best friend's greatest hour of need, carrying ammunition that could either save or damn them both.

Her heels clicked against marble steps as she climbed toward double doors that had welcomed generations of strong women who'd faced impossible choices. The entrance hall stretched before her like a cathedral—twelve-foot ceilings, crystal chandeliers that had witnessed Civil War secrets, Persian rugs that had cushioned the footsteps of women who'd survived everything history could inflict.

But none of those ancestral ghosts had ever faced the choice between protecting someone they loved and respecting their right to choose destruction.

The drawing room where Samantha retreated felt more like sanctuary than living space. Floor-to-ceiling windows overlooked gardens where camellias bloomed despite the approaching winter, their resilience mocking her current emotional fragility. Oil paintings of stern ancestors gazed down from gilded frames, their eyes seeming to judge her contemplation of betraying the very friendship they'd raised her to honor above all else.

She poured herself three fingers of bourbon—Pappy Van Winkle that had aged longer than some marriages lasted—and settled into the wingback chair where four generations of women had wrestled with moral dilemmas that had no clean solutions.

The envelope lay spread across her coffee table like tarot cards predicting multiple futures. Evidence that could destroy Dalvin Shaw completely. Financial records, drug transactions, photographs of affairs that would shatter political careers and social standings throughout New Orleans high society.

Shaniece, what are you asking me to do? Watch you sacrifice everything we've built because you believe mercy is more important than survival?

Her phone buzzed with messages she couldn't bring herself to read—probably other friends demanding to know what had happened at Commander's Palace, why she'd stormed out, whether their sisterhood was fracturing beyond repair. The vibrations felt like accusations against her thigh.

Outside, twilight painted the Garden District in shades of purple and gold that reminded her of countless evenings she and Shaniece had spent planning their futures on this very terrace. Dreams of business empires, perfect marriages, children who would inherit their legacies. Dreams that were crumbling under the weight of one man's cruelty and one woman's stubborn righteousness.

By 9 PM, Samantha had consumed enough bourbon to drown her inhibitions but not her convictions. The evidence demanded action. Every photograph, every financial record, every text message transcript screamed for justice that the legal system might never provide.

Shaniece, I love you too much to let you destroy yourself out of misplaced virtue.

She reached for her phone with fingers that trembled slightly, though it was unclear whether it was due to alcohol or emotion. Her contact list contained investigative journalists, television producers, social media influencers who could ensure Dalvin Shaw's destruction would be swift, thorough, and utterly devastating.

Marcus Chen at WDSU-TV had been investigating corruption in city government for months. One phone call would put this evidence in the hands of someone who could craft it into career-ending exposé that would dominate news cycles for weeks.

"Marcus? It's Samantha. I have information about City Council President Greg Maynard and his associates that could be very valuable to your investigation."

But as she began to dial, her phone exploded with emergency news alerts that made her bourbon-steadied hands freeze mid-motion:

BREAKING: CITY COUNCIL PRESIDENT'S WIFE QUESTIONED IN PATERNITY SCANDAL

DEVELOPING: Dina Maynard Pursued by Media Following DNA Test Results

EXCLUSIVE: "DIZ" IDENTIFIED IN MULTIPLE ADULTERY CASES INVOLVING POLITICAL FAMILIES

Divine Timing

The local news broadcast began with helicopter footage of Dina Maynard fleeing from reporters outside Ochsner Medical Center, her hospital gown flapping in artificial wind created by news choppers circling like mechanical vultures. The woman looked haggard, desperate, cornered by circumstances that had exploded beyond her control.

"Mrs. Maynard, is it true that your newborn son's father is Dalvin 'Diz' Shaw rather than your husband?" The reporter's voice carried through the chaos of clicking cameras and shouted questions.

"No comment! Leave me alone!" Dina's voice cracked with exhaustion and fear as security guards attempted to shield her from the media frenzy.

The news anchor's voice provided clinical narration over the chaos: "Sources close to the investigation report that DNA testing has confirmed Dalvin Shaw, known by his college nickname 'Diz,' as the biological father of infant James Maynard, born last week to City Council President Greg Maynard's wife, Dina."

Samantha's bourbon glass shattered against the marble floor as the full implications registered like earthquake tremors through her understanding of the situation.

"Furthermore, financial records obtained by investigators suggest a pattern of extramarital relationships involving Shaw and wives of several prominent political figures, including payments that may constitute blackmail or hush money."

The television screen filled with photographs she recognized—some identical to those in her envelope, others clearly obtained from different sources. Bank statements showing payments to multiple women. Hotel receipts spanning months of coordinated adultery. Text message screenshots revealing a web of deception that reached far beyond Shaniece's marriage.

"City Council President Maynard has scheduled an emergency press conference for tomorrow morning, while sources indicate that the District Attorney's office is reviewing evidence for potential criminal charges related to financial fraud and blackmail."

Her phone rang immediately—Margaux Morrison's number flashing urgently across the screen.

"Samantha, are you watching the news?"

"Every channel. How did this happen?"

"Dina Maynard apparently kept evidence of her own. When she discovered she was pregnant and Greg threatened divorce, she contacted other women who'd been involved with Dalvin. They compared notes, shared documentation, and took everything to a prosecutor who specializes in political corruption."

Through her drawing room windows, Samantha could see news vans beginning to gather at the end of her street—media sensing that anyone connected to this story might provide additional information or dramatic footage.

"What does this mean for Shaniece?"

"Vindication without participation. Dalvin's complete destruction without her fingerprints anywhere on the evidence. Divine justice, if you believe in such things."

The irony struck like lightning illuminating storm clouds. While she'd been wrestling with whether to betray her friend's principles for practical protection, God had been orchestrating justice through entirely different channels. Shaniece's choice to show mercy hadn't protected Dalvin—it had protected her own character while allowing divine timing to handle the destruction her conscience couldn't bear to inflict.

"Margaux, I need to call Shaniece."

"I suspect she's already watching. This changes everything—her divorce case, the financial recovery, her business protection. Dalvin won't survive this level of scandal, and she remains completely clean throughout his downfall."

The Uncomfortable Truth

Samantha's hands shook as she dialed Shaniece's number, her heart racing with mixture of relief, guilt, and desperate hope that their friendship could survive what she might have done. The phone rang three times before Shaniece answered with a voice that carried exhaustion mixed with something that might have been suspicion.

"Sam."

"Girl, I'm watching the news. Are you—"

"Did you do this?" The question cut through Samantha's attempted greeting like a blade through silk. No pleasantries, no deflection, just the direct confrontation she'd been dreading.

Silence stretched between them like a chasm neither wanted to acknowledge. Through her drawing room windows, Samantha could see news vans beginning to gather, their satellite dishes reaching toward storm clouds that seemed to mirror the tension crackling through the phone line.

"Shaniece, I—"

"Because if you released that information after I specifically asked you not to, then we have a much bigger problem than Dalvin's destruction. We have a trust issue that might be irreparable."

The pain in her friend's voice hit harder than any accusation. This wasn't anger—it was the devastation of someone who'd believed in her sister's integrity only to face potential betrayal at the moment of greatest vulnerability.

"I didn't release anything," Samantha replied, her voice barely above a whisper. "I was going to. I had my phone in my hand, ready to call Marcus Chen, when the news broke. But I didn't do this. I swear on everything we've built together—this wasn't me."

The silence that followed felt eternal. Samantha could hear news anchors in the background of Shaniece's call, their voices providing clinical narration of Dalvin's spectacular downfall while two sisters wrestled with questions of loyalty and trust.

"You swear?"

"I swear. On our friendship, on my mother's memory, on everything sacred between us—I didn't release this information. But Shaniece..." Her voice cracked with emotion she could no longer contain. "I almost did. I was so afraid of losing you to your own principles that I almost became someone who could betray them."

Another silence, shorter but somehow more profound. When Shaniece spoke again, her voice carried relief mixed with something deeper—forgiveness that had been prepared before the offense was even confirmed.

"I know you were scared. I know you think I was being naive or self-destructive. But Sam, if you had released that information, it would have changed me forever. Not just my reputation or my legal position—my soul."

Tears finally broke through Samantha's carefully constructed composure. "I almost destroyed us both because I couldn't trust that your way might actually work. I was so focused on protecting you that I nearly became the thing you needed protection from."

"But you didn't. When it mattered most, you chose to trust me even when you didn't understand me. That's what real love does—it respects the other person's right to make choices we wouldn't make ourselves."

Through her windows, Samantha watched more news vans arriving, their crews setting up equipment to capture whatever dramatic footage might emerge from the Garden District's response to scandal. But inside her ancestral home, reconciliation was blooming like camellias in winter—unexpected, beautiful, defiant of harsh conditions.

"Shaniece, watching this unfold...seeing divine justice happen without your fingerprints anywhere on the evidence...I'm beginning to understand what you meant about trusting God's timing over our own schemes."

"I wasn't wise, Sam. I was just scared that if I chose revenge over mercy, I'd become someone I couldn't live with. And honestly? I wasn't even sure I was making the right choice. I just knew it was the only choice I could make and still respect myself in the morning."

"Well, your obedience just taught me something about faith I've never understood before. Because watching you choose the harder path while I pushed for the easier one...see now that some battles are won through surrender rather than force."

They sat in comfortable silence for a moment, both watching identical news coverage from their respective homes while their friendship strengthened through philosophical understanding that had seemed impossible hours earlier.

"So what happens now?" Samantha asked.

"Now we watch God's justice unfold while we rebuild what matters most. Our friendship. My business. My faith. The things that actually survive when scandals fade and empires crumble."

"And I promise you," Samantha added with conviction that surprised them both, "the next time you choose the narrow path, I'll walk it with you instead of trying to push you toward the wide one."

As storm clouds finally opened to release rain that had been building all day, Samantha felt a cleansing wash over both the Garden District and her conscience. Divine intervention had solved moral dilemmas that human wisdom couldn't navigate, while preserving relationships that human schemes might have destroyed.

Thank you, she prayed silently, for protecting both my sister and our friendship when I almost failed them both.

CHAPTER 11: WHEN SISTERS DIVIDE

The lobby of Brooks, Bailey, & Solomon stretched before them like a battlefield dressed in marble and mahogany. Situated on the twenty-sixth floor of Place St. Charles, the law office had been the venue for New Orleans' legal elite to conduct their most sensitive business for over a century. Today, it would witness the kind of strategic warfare that legends were built upon.

Shaniece led the procession through revolving doors with the bearing of a general entering enemy territory. Behind her, Samantha moved with predatory grace, her Hermès briefcase containing financial ammunition that would reshape the morning's proceedings. Margaux Morrison followed—silver-haired and sharp as surgical steel, flanked by six additional attorneys whose combined billable hours could fund small nations.

The receptionist's practiced smile faltered when she recognized the convoy approaching her desk. Eight lawyers moving in formation meant someone's world was about to end.

"We're here for the emergency partners' meeting regarding the Dalvin Shaw matter," Margaux announced with a voice that could cut diamonds. "I believe our arrival is expected."

"I...let me call upstairs..."

"No need." Margaux's smile carried the warmth of an Antarctic wind. "We'll announce ourselves."

The War Room

Conference Room A occupied the corner of the twenty-sixth floor, its floor-to-ceiling windows offering commanding views of the Mississippi River where barges pushed against current like the legal system pushed against corruption. Inside, twelve senior partners of Louisiana's most prestigious law firm sat around a polished conference table, their faces bearing the strain of men discovering their golden goose was a poison pill.

Dalvin Shaw slouched at the far end, his usual swagger replaced by desperate calculation. The news coverage had stripped away his carefully constructed image, revealing the hollow man beneath designer suits and professional accomplishments. His bloodshot eyes darted between partners who no longer met his gaze with respect or recognition.

"Gentlemen," Senior Partner Harrison Brooks addressed the room with voice carrying sixty years of courtroom authority, "we need to discuss immediate damage control regarding recent...revelations about Mr. Shaw's personal conduct and its potential impact on firm reputation."

"Impact?" Partner James Bailey's voice cracked with barely controlled panic. "Harrison, we're facing potential criminal conspiracy charges if prosecutors determine we facilitated or enabled his financial misconduct."

The massive double doors exploded inward with force that rattled the crystal water glasses and sent legal pads scattering. The sound echoed through the conference room like thunder announcing divine judgment, causing twelve senior partners to jolt upright in their leather chairs.

Margaux Morrison swept through the entrance first, her silver hair catching light like a crown as she surveyed the room with the expression of a queen entering conquered territory. Her six-attorney entourage filed in behind her, briefcases clicking against marble floors like the measured steps of an execution squad.

"Gentlemen," Margaux announced, her voice carrying the authority of someone who'd just shifted the balance of power permanently, "I do hope we're not interrupting anything important. Although I suspect what we have to discuss will prove far more significant than whatever ... damage control you were attempting."

Shaniece entered next, her midnight blue Valentino blazer cut to perfection over matching silk trousers, the ensemble commanding respect while suggesting she'd dressed for war rather than negotiation. She moved with the controlled grace of someone who'd learned to command boardrooms across three continents, her presence transforming the space from crisis meeting to tribunal.

But it was Samantha's entrance that electrified the atmosphere. She paused in the doorway, allowing her gaze to sweep across the assembled partners before settling on Dalvin with the focused intensity of a predator selecting prey. Her Hermès briefcase swung from her hand like a medieval war hammer as she strutted—there was no other word for it—to the conference table.

"Well, well, well." Her voice carried theatrical amusement that made several partners visibly uncomfortable. "If it isn't the infamous Dalvin Shaw. Or should I say 'Diz'? I've heard so much about your ... extracurricular activities."

Dalvin's face flushed red as embarrassment and rage warred for control. "You have no right to be here. This is a private partners' meeting—"

"Private?" Samantha's laugh could have cut glass. "Honey, after this week's news cycle, your private life has become New Orleans' favorite entertainment. I particularly enjoyed the helicopter footage of your baby mama running from reporters. Very dignified."

"Samantha, perhaps we should—" Shaniece began diplomatically.

"Oh no, baby girl. I've been waiting for this moment." Samantha's smile revealed teeth that seemed sharper than usual. "Dalvin, I have to ask—when you were systematically stealing from my best friend, did it occur to you that she might have friends who don't forgive and forget quite as easily as she does?"

"I never stole anything," Dalvin protested, though his voice lacked conviction. "Those were marital assets, legally accessible—"

"Legally accessible?" Samantha's eyebrows rose so high they nearly disappeared into her hairline. "Is that what we're calling embezzlement now? How refreshingly creative. Tell me, did Brooks, Bailey & Solomon teach you that particular interpretation of marital law, or did you develop that theory independently while high on whatever substances you've been using?"

The room fell silent except for the tick of an antique grandfather clock that seemed to be counting down to someone's professional execution. Several partners exchanged glances that spoke of men realizing their golden parachutes had just transformed into concrete anchors.

"What is the meaning of this intrusion?" Harrison Brooks demanded, though his voice carried less authority than a substitute teacher facing unruly teenagers.

Margaux smiled with the warmth of a blizzard in January. "Justice, Harrison. Something that appears to be in critically short supply within these hallowed halls."

Samantha opened her briefcase with the precision of a surgeon, revealing diseased organs. Financial documents cascaded across mahogany surface—bank statements, wire transfers, investment records that painted devastating pictures of systematic embezzlement orchestrated from within the law firm's own offices.

"For the past eighteen months," Margaux began, her voice gaining power like a gathering storm, "your associate Mr. Shaw has been systematically draining assets belonging to Hermosa Industries through fraudulent legal instruments, forged documents, and unauthorized financial transactions."

Partner David Solomon reached for the nearest document, his face growing pale as implications became clear. "These transactions ... they bear our firm's letterhead. Our clients' trust account numbers."

"Indeed they do." Margaux's smile could have frozen champagne. "Which creates fascinating legal questions about institutional liability when associates use firm resources to commit fraud against other clients."

Dalvin shot to his feet, his chair scraping against hardwood like fingernails on chalkboards. "This is harassment! These documents could be fabricated—"

"Sit down and shut up," Samantha screeched with a voice that could stop traffic. "The adults are talking, and your opinion is no longer relevant to these proceedings."

The room fell silent except for air conditioning humming and papers rustling as partners discovered the scope of financial devastation perpetrated under their professional supervision.

"The damage to Hermosa Industries exceeds forty-seven million dollars," Margaux continued, spreading additional evidence like playing cards revealing royal flush. "Wire transfers from joint accounts, liquidation of shared investments, fraudulent loans secured against company assets—all orchestrated through legal instruments bearing this firm's official seals."

Harrison Brooks studied documents with growing horror. "Dalvin, please tell me you didn't use our trust accounts for personal transactions."

"I ... the accounts were legally accessible through marital asset provisions..."

"You used client funds for personal speculation?" James Bailey's voice rose to near-hysteria. "Do you understand what this means for our professional licenses? Our malpractice insurance? Our criminal liability?"

Margaux allowed silence to build while partners contemplated the magnitude of professional and personal destruction facing them. When she spoke again, her voice carried finality that left no room for negotiation.

"We demand immediate restitution of two times actual damages—ninety-four million dollars—to compensate for lost business opportunities, reputation damage, and punitive measures warranted by institutional negligence."

Shaniece stepped forward, her presence commanding attention from men who'd spent careers underestimating women in boardrooms. "Actually, I just want to be made whole. Hermosa needs restoration, not revenge."

"Absolutely not," Samantha interrupted with conviction that surprised everyone present. "God is a God of abundance, not scarcity. Proverbs 6:31 says clearly: 'When the thief is found, he shall restore sevenfold.' This isn't about revenge—this is about biblical justice."

Margaux nodded approvingly. "Mrs. Williams has cited applicable precedent. Biblical law requires complete restoration plus penalty for willful theft. In this case, sevenfold restitution equals three hundred twenty-nine million dollars."

The conference room erupted in protests, demands for reasonableness, threats of counter-litigation that everyone knew would fail under scrutiny. Partners who'd spent careers intimidating opponents now faced opponents who couldn't be intimidated.

"That's impossible," Harrison Brooks protested. "The firm doesn't possess that level of liquid assets."

"Then you'll liquidate everything—real estate, investments, partnerships, retirement accounts—until biblical restitution is achieved," Margaux replied with a smile that could melt steel. "Or we'll pursue criminal conspiracy charges, professional misconduct complaints, and civil litigation that will destroy this institution completely."

David Solomon grabbed Harrison's arm. "Harrison, we need to discuss this privately. The criminal exposure alone ..."

"You have fifteen minutes to accept our terms," Margaux announced, checking her Cartier watch with theatrical precision. "After that, we file papers with the District Attorney's office and the Louisiana State Bar Association simultaneously."

Checkmate

The partners huddled in desperate whispered conversations while Dalvin sat frozen like deer caught in headlights. His world was collapsing in real time—career, reputation, marriage, freedom, all evaporating under the weight of consequences he'd never imagined possible.

"We'll need to structure payments over time," Harrison Brooks finally admitted defeat. "Liquidating the firm's assets will take months."

"Sixty days for initial payment of one hundred million," Margaux countered without mercy. "Remaining balance over eighteen months with interest. Miss any payment, and we pursue criminal charges while seizing all remaining assets."

"That's financial murder," James Bailey protested.

"That's justice," Samantha replied. "Biblical justice that recognizes theft demands not only restitution, but a penalty severe enough to deter future misconduct."

David Solomon cleared his throat, his voice carrying the resignation of a man calculating inevitable losses. "Harrison, we need to be practical here. The discretionary fund contains approximately four hundred million in liquid assets—partnership distributions, contingency reserves, and settlement proceeds from the Petrochemical class action. We could pay this in full today and require a comprehensive non-disclosure agreement from all parties."

The suggestion hung in the air like smoke from expensive cigars, each partner mentally calculating their personal financial devastation against the alternative of criminal prosecution and professional annihilation.

"David raises a valid point," another partner murmured reluctantly. "Clean break, immediate resolution, sealed records. Better than years of litigation that destroys what's left of our reputation."

Harrison Brooks's face cycled through stages of grief—denial, anger, bargaining—before settling on grim acceptance. "And we'd walk away from this intact?"

Margaux exchanged glances with her legal team before responding. "Full payment within forty-eight hours, comprehensive NDA covering all parties, and Mr. Shaw's immediate termination with cause. Those terms would resolve our civil claims entirely."

Shaniece watched the proceedings with mixture of amazement and discomfort. The devastation being visited upon this institution felt simultaneously satisfying and overwhelming. These men who'd enabled Dalvin's destruction of her life now faced their own professional annihilation.

Lord, is this really Your justice, or is this human revenge dressed in biblical language?

But watching Dalvin's face crumble as he realized the complete scope of his defeat, she felt something she hadn't expected: not satisfaction, but pity. He'd destroyed himself more thoroughly than any external force could have managed.

Harrison Brooks signed settlement documents with hands that shook like autumn leaves. "This will bankrupt the firm within two years."

"Then you should have chosen your associates more carefully," Margaux replied without sympathy. "Professional responsibility includes accountability for institutional culture that enables misconduct. And I am sure you have money hidden somewhere hidden in your books anyway."

As quickly as they'd arrived, Shaniece's legal army gathered their documents and prepared to depart. Victory achieved through overwhelming force and biblical precedent, leaving behind professional carnage that would reshape Louisiana's legal landscape.

"One final matter," Margaux addressed the room with a tone of absolute authority. "Mr. Shaw's access to firm resources, trust accounts, and professional systems terminates immediately. Security will escort him from the building, and any attempt to contact our client or interfere with Hermosa Industries will result in criminal charges and contempt of court proceedings."

Dalvin remained seated, staring at settlement documents that spelled out the complete destruction of everything he'd worked to build. Forty-seven years of life reduced to cautionary tales about the consequences of betraying trust and choosing destruction over integrity.

"Dalvin," Shaniece said quietly, her voice carrying compassion despite everything he'd put her through. "I hope you find help. I hope you find healing. But I also hope you understand that choices have consequences, and some consequences are irreversible."

She turned toward the door, then paused. "And I forgive you. Not because you deserve it, but because I refuse to carry hatred that would poison my future."

The legal convoy departed Brooks, Bailey, & Solomon like storm clouds moving toward different horizons, leaving behind wreckage that would take years to rebuild and reputations that would never fully recover.

In the elevator descending toward street level, Samantha turned to her dearest friend with an expression mixed with awe and affection. "Girl, watching you extend mercy while demanding justice ... that was masterful. Biblical justice that protects other potential victims while maintaining your spiritual integrity. Who would've thought?"

"I still feel uncomfortable with the severity," Shaniece admitted. "Three hundred twenty-nine million dollars will destroy more lives than just Dalvin's."

"Sometimes justice requires consequences severe enough to prevent future misconduct," Margaux observed. "You've protected not only your interests, but every future client who might have been victimized by institutional negligence."

As they emerged onto bustling New Orleans streets where life continued despite personal earthquakes reshaping individual worlds, Shaniece felt a strange mixture of vindication and exhaustion. Divine justice had been served through earthly systems, but the cost in human terms felt staggering.

Thank You, Lord, for providing restoration beyond what I could have imagined. Help me use this abundance for Your glory rather than personal satisfaction.

The war was over. Victory achieved. Justice served with biblical exactness.

But somehow, she suspected the real work was just beginning.

CHAPTER 12: DANGEROUS REVELATIONS

The Gathering Storm

The private dining room at Arnaud's French 75 Bar felt more like a diplomatic summit than a sisterly reunion. Shaniece had chosen the intimate setting hoping familiar surroundings might ease the tensions that had fractured their circle, but the crystal chandelier seemed to cast harsh light on relationships strained beyond their natural flexibility.

Samantha arrived first, her burgundy Yves Saint Laurent blazer suggesting she'd dressed for battle disguised as business lunch. She claimed the seat closest to where Shaniece would sit—protective positioning that hadn't gone unnoticed by the others trickling in with varying degrees of enthusiasm and reluctance.

Renee entered wearing a black Chanel suit that made her look like she was attending a funeral—perhaps an appropriate choice given the state of their sisterhood. Her recent divorce had carved harsh lines around her eyes, transforming the vibrant woman they'd known into someone who seemed to view the world through lenses of disappointment and betrayal.

Moni and Coko arrived together, their synchronized entrance speaking of private conversations and shared concerns about the gathering they were about to witness. Both wore neutral colors that suggested diplomatic intentions—beige and cream ensembles that wouldn't take sides in whatever conflict was brewing.

Trange' swept in last, her red Valentino dress announcing her presence like a declaration of war. She'd chosen to make a statement, and that statement was clear: she refused to apologize for practical wisdom in a world that punished idealistic foolishness.

"Ladies," Shaniece began once they'd settled around the mahogany table that had witnessed countless New Orleans power brokers negotiate their own treaties and truces. "I asked you all here because our friendship deserves better than the way we left things at Commander's Palace."

"Does it?" Trange' interrupted, her voice carrying the sharp edge of someone who'd been rehearsing this conversation. "Because I'm still trying to understand how biblical principles suddenly became more important than loyalty to the women who've stood by you for decades."

The opening salvo struck its target. Shaniece felt the familiar tightening in her chest that came with defending choices she'd made from spiritual conviction rather than worldly wisdom.

"My principles didn't replace our friendship, Trange'. They protected me from becoming someone who could destroy others to save herself. There's a difference."

"Is there?" Renee's voice carried a bitter tone that made everyone uncomfortable. "Because from where I'm sitting, your mercy toward Dalvin looks exactly like the mistake I made with Marvin. High-minded forgiveness that enabled continued abuse while the abuser faced no real consequences."

Samantha leaned forward, her protective instincts flaring. "Renee, with respect, Shaniece's situation worked out differently than yours. Divine justice handled Dalvin more thoroughly than any revenge scheme could have managed."

"Divine justice?" Trange' laughed burst forth with a sound like breaking glass. "You mean coincidence and other people's courage to act when she wouldn't. If those women hadn't come forward about Dalvin's affairs, he'd still be destroying her business while she prayed for his redemption."

The accusation hung in the air like smoke from expensive cigars, choking the atmosphere with implications none of them wanted to fully examine.

Moni cleared her throat, her usual diplomatic nature warring with growing frustration. "Can I ask something that's been bothering me? Trange', why are you even here? You've made it clear you don't respect Shaniece's choices or understand our friendship dynamics. What exactly are you hoping to accomplish?"

The question struck like lightning illuminating storm clouds. Everyone had been thinking it, but only Moni possessed sufficient courage—or perhaps sufficient irritation—to voice what others had merely whispered in private conversations.

Trange' straightened in her chair, red dress blazing like armor against diplomatic attacks. "I'm here because someone needs to represent reality in a room full of people who've confused enabling with loyalty. Samantha's protecting someone who nearly destroyed herself through spiritual stubbornness. The rest of you are pretending that friendship means supporting every decision, even when those decisions are objectively self-destructive."

"That's enough," Samantha declared, her voice carrying a warning that made several nearby diners glance toward their table.

"No, it's *not* enough." Trange' stood partially, her movement suggesting she was prepared for whatever confrontation might follow. "You've all been walking on eggshells around Saint Shaniece and her newfound religious convictions, but I'm not going to pretend that choosing abstract principles over concrete loyalty represents some kind of spiritual evolution."

Samantha rose from her chair with fluid motion that somehow conveyed both elegance and menace. "You need to check yourself right now. Shaniece showed more courage choosing the narrow path than you've shown in your entire life of taking easy roads that require no moral backbone."

"Moral backbone?" Trange' stood fully, her height advantage lost to Samantha's presence that seemed to expand beyond physical dimensions. "I call it moral cowardice. Hiding behind religious platitudes to avoid making hard decisions that might require getting your hands dirty."

The space between them crackled with electricity that had nothing to do with the restaurant's atmospheric lighting. Other diners began noticing the tension, their conversations dropping to whispers as they sensed drama unfolding at the corner table.

"Ladies," Coko intervened desperately, "we're in public. People are staring."

But neither woman seemed inclined toward de-escalation. Years of philosophical differences, personality conflicts, and competing loyalties had crystallized into this moment where civil discourse threatened to dissolve into something far more primitive.

"You want to talk about dirty hands?" Samantha's voice dropped to a dangerous whisper that somehow carried more menace than shouting. "My hands stayed clean while divine justice destroyed Dalvin more completely than any human scheme. Your hands would have been covered in blood that accomplished nothing except temporary satisfaction."

"And your friend would have been financially ruined while you prayed over her corpse," Trange' shot back with equal venom.

"ENOUGH."

Shaniece's voice cut through their confrontation with authority that reminded everyone why she'd built a billion-dollar empire before turning thirty-five. The single word carried enough power to silence not just her friends but half the restaurant.

She stood slowly, her midnight blue Valentino blazer seeming to absorb light as she positioned herself between potential combatants. "This ends *now*. Both of you sit down before I make decisions about this friendship that none of us want to live with."

Coko seized the moment of stunned silence to assert diplomatic authority she rarely displayed in group dynamics. "Everyone sit. Now. We're going to have this conversation like the educated, successful women we are instead of reality TV stars fighting over camera time."

Her unexpected firmness accomplished what pleading couldn't—both Samantha and Trange' resumed their seats, though their postures suggested truces rather than surrenders.

"Here's what I see," Coko continued, her voice gaining strength from necessity. "Trange', your concerns weren't wrong. Shaniece was taking enormous risks by refusing to fight back with available weapons. But your delivery is poisonous, and your inability to understand spiritual conviction makes you sound like someone who's never wrestled with moral decisions harder than choosing between designer handbags."

Trange' opened her mouth to protest, but Coko's raised hand stopped her.

"Samantha, your loyalty is beautiful, but your willingness to escalate to physical violence over philosophical disagreement suggests you've forgotten that protecting someone includes protecting them from your own worst impulses."

She turned to Shaniece with expression mixing affection and exasperation. "As for you, sister girl, your spiritual journey is genuine and admirable. But expecting everyone to understand or support decisions they didn't help make creates impossible situations for people who love you enough to worry about your well-being."

The diagnosis felt surgical in its accuracy. Each woman recognized uncomfortable truths about her own behavior while grappling with equally uncomfortable truths about the others.

"So, what's the solution?" Renee asked, her bitterness temporarily displaced by curiosity about whether their fractured sisterhood could be repaired.

"Honesty," Coko replied simply. "Trange', if you can't respect Shaniece's spiritual choices, then maybe this friendship has run its course. But if you can disagree without being disagreeable, then we work through this. Samantha, you support Shaniece without attacking everyone who questions her methods. And Shaniece, you accept that spiritual conviction doesn't make you immune from loving criticism."

Silence settled over their table like dust after an explosion, each woman processing the mediator's assessment of their collective dysfunction. The restaurant's ambient noise—clinking glasses, muted conversations, soft jazz from the bar area—seemed to provide cover for internal negotiations none of them had expected to conduct.

Trange' spoke first, her voice stripped of earlier venom but still carrying reservation. "I can disagree without being cruel. But I won't pretend to understand choices that seem designed to maximize suffering for the sake of spiritual purity. That's not friendship—that's enablement of self-destruction."

"And I won't pretend that practical wisdom justifies abandoning moral conviction the moment it becomes inconvenient," Shaniece replied, her tone matching Trange's careful neutrality. "But I can accept that my choices affect people who love me, and their concerns deserve respect even when I can't follow their advice."

Samantha nodded reluctantly. "I can support you without attacking everyone who questions your methods. But I won't apologize for being willing to fight for someone who won't fight for herself. That's what family does."

"Fair enough," Trange' conceded. "But we're agreeing to disagree, not pretending our philosophical differences have disappeared. I still think spiritual idealism is dangerous when predators are circling. You still think practical realism is morally bankrupt. We both might be right."

The acknowledgment felt less like reconciliation than diplomatic cease-fire, but cease-fires had their own value when the alternative was permanent war.

Renee had remained silent throughout the negotiation, her expression cycling between envy and skepticism as she watched her friends find paths toward understanding that remained elusive in her own spiritual journey.

"Must be nice," she said finally, "having faith strong enough to trust divine justice when human justice fails. Some of us don't have that luxury."

Shaniece reached across the table, her hand covering Renee's with gentle pressure. "The luxury isn't faith, sister. It's surrender. Letting go of the burden of orchestrating other people's consequences while focusing on your own healing. It's harder than revenge, but it's also more freeing."

"Is it?" Renee's voice carried the weight of someone who'd chosen bitterness over forgiveness and was discovering the true cost of that choice. "Because from where I'm sitting, my bitterness feels more honest than your forgiveness. At least I'm not pretending that mercy magically heals wounds that deserve to stay open."

The conversation had shifted from philosophical disagreement to spiritual diagnosis, with Renee's pain serving as a case study for the long-term effects of choosing revenge over restoration. Her recent divorce had provided temporary satisfaction—Marvin faced social embarrassment and financial consequences—but the victory had left her more isolated and bitter than she'd anticipated.

"Renee," Shaniece said gently, "your wounds deserve acknowledgement and care. But keeping them open doesn't honor your pain—it perpetuates it. Forgiveness isn't about pretending damage didn't happen. It's about refusing to let that damage define your future."

"Easy words from someone whose divine justice delivered complete vindication," Renee replied, though her voice carried more exhaustion than anger. "Try forgiving when the person who destroyed you walks away with half your assets and a new boyfriend while you're left rebuilding from nothing."

"That's exactly when forgiveness becomes most powerful," Shaniece countered. "When it costs everything and offers no immediate benefits except freedom from carrying poison that's destroying you from within."

The spiritual counseling session had transformed their lunch into something none of them had expected—a moment when surface conflicts revealed deeper questions about faith, justice, and the price of choosing different paths through betrayal and loss.

Moni and Coko exchanged glances that spoke of women recognizing they were witnessing something more significant than friendship repair. They were watching spiritual warfare play out in real time, with each woman representing different responses to the fundamental question of how to survive when life's most important relationships explode without warning.

The lunch concluded with tentative hugs and promises to "do better" that carried hope mixed with skepticism. Trange' left first, her red Valentino still making statements about refusing to apologize for practical wisdom. Renee followed, her black Chanel suggesting she wasn't ready to abandon mourning for optimism.

Moni and Coko departed together, their diplomatic mission partially successful but requiring ongoing maintenance to prevent future explosions. They'd brokered a truce, not a peace treaty.

Samantha and Shaniece remained at the table, sharing the comfortable silence of sisters who'd survived another test of their bond.

"Think it'll hold?" Samantha asked, gesturing toward the door through which their friends had departed.

"The truce? Maybe. But Renee's going to need something more than friendship to heal what's eating her alive. And Trange' ... I'm not sure we can bridge the gap between spiritual conviction and practical cynicism."

"Maybe that's okay," Samantha mused. "Maybe some relationships are meant to survive disagreement rather than require agreement. As long as we love each other enough to keep showing up, the rest might work itself out."

They paid their check and prepared to leave Arnaud's, where diplomatic negotiations had produced mixed results but maintained hope for something better than permanent estrangement.

As they stepped onto Royal Street, afternoon sunlight painted the French Quarter in golden hues that made even ordinary buildings look touched by divine artistry. New Orleans continued its eternal dance between sacred and secular, tourist attraction and authentic culture, hope and disappointment—much like the friendships they were all trying to navigate.

"I'm proud of the way you handled that," Samantha said as they prepared to part ways. "Trange' was looking for a fight, and you gave her grace instead."

"Grace is easier when you're walking in victory," Shaniece replied. "The real test comes when you're in the valley and grace feels like the last thing you want to offer."

The Unexpected Visitor

The drive to her Garden District home provided time for reflection on conversations that had revealed as much about her own spiritual journey as about the fractures in her friendships. Forgiveness was easier to preach than practice, mercy more comfortable to discuss than deliver, and grace felt most natural when offered from positions of strength rather than vulnerability.

Her circular driveway welcomed her Mercedes with familiar silence, Spanish moss draping ancient oaks like nature's own cathedral. The antebellum mansion rose before her like sanctuary after hours of emotional warfare disguised as sisterly lunch.

But as she approached her front door, keys jingling in the evening air, movement in the shadows caused her to freeze midstep. A figure emerged from the darkness beside her wraparound porch—a woman holding something that looked like a bundle of fabric until the bundle shifted and revealed tiny arms reaching toward the streetlight.

"Shaniece." Dina Maynard's voice cracked with exhaustion and desperation. "Please don't run. I need to talk to you."

The woman who'd unknowingly become instrumental in Dalvin's destruction stood trembling in the gathering dusk, her hospital bracelet still visible on her wrist, her newborn son cradled against her chest like hope wrapped in receiving blankets.

"Dina? What are you doing here? How did you even—"

"I know this is crazy," Dina interrupted, her words tumbling over each other with urgency born of desperation. "But you're the only person who might understand. You're the only other woman who knows what Dalvin really is underneath all the charm and lies."

The infant stirred in her arms, tiny face scrunching with the universal expression of newborns discovering the world outside the womb wasn't as comfortable as promised. In that moment, looking at mother and child silhouetted against her porch light, Shaniece saw her own story reflected in different choices and consequences.

Lord, what are You asking of me now?

CHAPTER 13: THE CALVARY AND CALVARY

"Come inside."

The words escaped Shaniece's lips before rational thought could intervene. Part pity, part curiosity, but mostly something deeper—recognition of shared wounds that transcended their complicated history. "You and the baby shouldn't be standing out here in the evening air."

Dina's relief was palpable as she clutched her newborn closer, following Shaniece through the mahogany double doors into a world that existed on an entirely different economic plane than anything she'd experienced. The marble foyer stretched before them like a museum exhibition, with crystal chandeliers casting prismatic light across Persian rugs that probably cost more than most people's annual salaries.

"My God," Dina whispered, her voice echoing in the cavernous space. "I knew you were successful, but this ..."

Shaniece felt momentarily uncomfortable viewing her home through the eyes of someone who'd never possessed such abundance. The imported Italian marble, the hand-painted ceiling murals, the antique furnishings that had been collected over years of international business travel—it all seemed excessive when witnessed by someone holding a baby while wearing clothes that had clearly been slept in.

"Let's sit in the living room," Shaniece suggested, leading Dina through archways that opened onto spaces designed for entertaining heads of state rather than intimate conversations with desperate young mothers.

The living room commanded respect with floor-to-ceiling windows overlooking manicured gardens where century-old live oaks created natural cathedrals. French silk upholstery in cream and gold created seating arrangements that could accommodate dozens, while original oil paintings by masters whose names appeared in art history textbooks gazed down from walls that had witnessed negotiations involving millions of dollars.

Dina sank into a chair that probably cost more than her monthly rent, her eyes scanning surroundings that seemed to overwhelm rather than comfort. "This is like something from magazines. I can't even imagine living like this."

The baby stirred in Dina's arms, making soft sounds that pierced through Shaniece's carefully constructed emotional barriers like arrows finding their mark. Tiny fingers grasped at air while a perfect little face scrunched with the universal expression of infants discovering the world beyond the womb.

He's beautiful, Shaniece thought, then immediately felt the familiar ache that accompanied any encounter with newborns—the reminder of what she'd lost at seventeen, what Dalvin's violence had stolen from her just months ago, what she would never experience no matter how much wealth or success she accumulated.

"I ... excuse me for a moment," she managed, her voice tightening with emotion she couldn't suppress. "Can I get you something to drink? Water, tea?"

"Water would be wonderful," Dina replied, clearly sensing the shift in atmosphere but not understanding its source.

Shaniece escaped to her gourmet kitchen, where stainless steel appliances and granite countertops provided cold comfort against the wave of grief washing over her. She'd thought she'd processed the infertility, accepted it as part of God's plan for her life, but seeing Dalvin's son—healthy, perfect, everything she'd dreamed of creating—reopened wounds that had never fully healed.

Lord, I know You have purposes I can't understand, but this hurts more than I expected. Help me focus on this woman's need rather than my own pain.

While Shaniece composed herself in the kitchen, Dina's eyes continued their systematic exploration of surroundings that felt more like visiting European palaces than American homes. Everything spoke of careful curation—from the Baccarat crystal collection displayed in custom cabinets to the fresh orchids that appeared to be professionally maintained.

The baby began to fuss, his small cries echoing through rooms designed for acoustics that enhanced rather than muffled sound. Dina stood carefully, walking toward the windows where moonlight streamed across gardens that looked professionally landscaped even in darkness.

This could have been my life, she thought with a mixture of envy and sadness. *If Dalvin had kept his promises, if the plan had worked, if he'd been the man he pretended to be.*

But even as the fantasy played through her mind, reality reasserted itself. The luxury surrounding her felt cold despite its beauty, isolated despite its impressiveness. Money had created paradise, but paradise felt empty when experienced alone.

Family photographs on side tables caught her attention—images of Shaniece with an older woman who must have been her mother, pictures from business events where she commanded rooms full of powerful people, vacation shots from exotic locations that spoke of freedom to travel anywhere in the world.

Yet conspicuously absent were the photos Dina had expected to find: pictures of Shaniece and Dalvin together, romantic shots from their marriage, evidence of the love story that had supposedly justified the destruction of other relationships.

Maybe their marriage was already over before I came along, she realized with dawning understanding. Maybe I was a convenient excuse for something that was dying anyway.

The Truth Unveiled

Shaniece returned with crystal glasses filled with ice water, her composure restored through prayer and determination. She settled into the chair across from Dina, maintaining a distance that felt safe while close enough for intimate conversation.

"Tell me why you're here," she said gently. "And please, start from the beginning."

Dina adjusted the baby against her shoulder, gathering courage to reveal truths that would shatter whatever illusions remained about the man they'd both loved in different ways.

"Dalvin told me his marriage was over months before we ... before anything happened between us," she began, her voice barely above a whisper. "He said you'd grown apart, that you were more focused on business than being a wife, that he was lonely and needed someone who understood him."

The words stung despite Shaniece's preparation for painful revelations. Every affair began with similar justifications—the neglected husband, the distant wife, the loneliness that supposedly justified betrayal.

"When I got pregnant, we made plans," Dina continued, her voice growing stronger with confession. "He was going to leave you after securing some business deal that would set us up financially. I was going to leave Greg once the divorce papers were filed.

We talked about getting married, raising the baby together, starting fresh."

"But that's not what happened."

"No." Dina's voice cracked with emotion. "Everything changed when Dalvin got involved with some men who … who weren't the kind of business associates you'd expect someone like him to know."

Shaniece felt ice forming in her stomach as implications began crystallizing. "What kind of men?"

"Dangerous men. Men who loan money to people who can't get it through legitimate channels, who expect payment regardless of circumstances, who don't accept excuses about market downturns or business setbacks."

The baby began crying in earnest, sensing his mother's distress through mechanisms that science couldn't fully explain. Dina bounced him gently while continuing her narrative, maternal instinct competing with desperate need to share information that might save both their lives.

"Dalvin borrowed money to finance some underground operation—something about importing goods that couldn't be brought in through normal channels. He promised huge returns, guaranteed profits that would solve all our problems."

"How much money?" Shaniece asked, though she dreaded the answer.

"Two million. Maybe more. I never got exact numbers, but enough that when the operation failed, these men started making threats about collecting from anyone connected to him."

The story that emerged painted a picture of Dalvin Shaw that bore no resemblance to the man Shaniece had married fifteen years earlier. This version was reckless, desperate, willing to endanger not just himself but everyone around him to finance get-rich-quick schemes that appealed to his gambling instincts.

"When they started threatening me and the baby, I went to the District Attorney," Dina explained, her voice shaking with remembered fear. "I figured if I gave them everything I knew about Dalvin's affairs, his financial misconduct, his connections to these dangerous men, maybe they'd provide protection in exchange for testimony."

"That's how all the evidence became public."

"Yes, but somehow these men found out I'd gone to the authorities. Last week, someone attacked me in the hospital parking garage. If security hadn't been nearby..." She trailed off, the implications clear enough without elaboration.

Shaniece felt the familiar tightening in her chest that accompanied recognition of genuine danger. The comfortable distance she'd maintained from Dalvin's destruction was evaporating as she realized his criminal associations might not distinguish between ex-wives and current targets.

"Dalvin disappeared the day after the news broke," Dina continued. "No contact, no explanation, no concern for what might happen to us. These men are still looking for their money, and they don't care who they collect it from."

"What about your husband? Surely Greg has resources to protect you."

Dina's laugh carried no humor whatsoever. "Greg is done with me. Publicly humiliated, politically destroyed, socially ostracized. He wants nothing to do with me or the baby. I'm on my own with nowhere to turn and people looking for me who don't make idle threats."

The weight of realization settled over Shaniece like fog rolling in from the Gulf. She wasn't just dealing with the aftermath of a messy divorce—she was potentially in danger from criminals who viewed her vast wealth as compensation for Dalvin's unpaid debts.

"I'm leaving the country," Dina announced with finality that suggested decisions already made. "Tonight. I have a sister in Canada who can help us disappear until this blows over or these men find someone else to blame."

"Why are you telling me this?"

"Because you need to know what you're dealing with. These aren't white-collar criminals who respect boundaries or legal proceedings. They're people who solve problems through violence, and right now, you represent the biggest potential source of recovery for money they'll never see from Dalvin."

Divine Wisdom Through Human Resources

Fear rose in Shaniece's throat like bile, but alongside the fear came clarity born of spiritual maturity that had learned to recognize divine guidance even in moments of crisis. God would protect her, but He also provided wisdom about practical steps required for that protection.

I know exactly who to call.

"Dina, thank you for warning me. That took courage, especially considering everything that's happened between us."

"I never meant for any of this to happen," Dina whispered, tears finally breaking through emotional barriers she'd maintained throughout her confession. "I know that doesn't excuse anything, but I thought I was in love with someone who loved me back. I never imagined I was a convenient distraction for a man who was willing to destroy everyone around him."

Shaniece moved to the window, pulling out her phone while gazing across gardens that had always represented peace and security but now felt exposed and vulnerable. Two contacts appeared on her screen—women she'd argued with just hours earlier, whose husbands possessed exactly the expertise this situation required.

"Coko? I know we just left each other, but I need help. Can you and your husband come to my house immediately? And call Moni—I need her husband here too. It's an emergency involving personal security."

The conversation lasted less than three minutes, but by its conclusion, Shaniece knew that military-trained professionals would be assessing her home's vulnerabilities within the hour. Marcus and David had built their security company on principles learned in Special Forces operations, and they'd treated her like family since marrying her closest friends.

Thank You, Lord, for providing protectors even when I didn't know I needed protection. Help me trust Your provision while taking responsible action.

As she ended the call, she turned back to Dina, who was preparing to leave for a journey that might save her life but would certainly change it forever.

"Go," Shaniece said simply. "Get your son to safety. And Dina? I forgive you. For all of it. You were as much a victim as a participant in whatever Dalvin was orchestrating."

The words surprised them both with their sincerity and power. In the space of one conversation, enemies had become allies united by shared recognition of the man they'd both loved—and the danger he'd created for everyone who'd trusted him.

As Dina disappeared into the night with her infant son, Shaniece began preparing for a different kind of battle than she'd ever imagined fighting. This wouldn't be won in boardrooms or courtrooms—this would require the kind of protective wisdom that recognized divine provision often came through very human resources.

Lord, I'm learning that trusting You doesn't mean being passive. Sometimes faith requires calling in the cavalry.

CHAPTER 14: THE TRAP SPRINGS

When Two Worlds Collide

The sound of multiple vehicles in Shaniece's circular driveway announced the coming of reinforcements she'd never imagined needing. Through her front windows, she watched two black SUVs discharge their passengers with systematic efficiency—Marcus and David emerging first, their arrival immediately transforming her peaceful Garden District sanctuary into something resembling a tactical operations center.

Behind them came Moni and Coko, their faces mixing concern for their friend with the particular worry that accompanied watching their husbands shift into combat mode. The four people approaching her door represented the convergence of two very different worlds: one born from military action, the other grounded in religious principle.

"Thank you for coming so quickly," Shaniece said as she ushered them inside, noting how Marcus and David's eyes immediately began cataloging sight lines, entry points, and potential vulnerabilities that had never occurred to her during fifteen years of living in supposed security.

"When family calls, we respond," Marcus replied, his voice carrying the authority of someone accustomed to life-and-death decisions. At six-foot-two with shoulders that suggested serious gym time, he commanded respect even in civilian clothes. "Tell us exactly what we're dealing with."

The next thirty minutes resembled a military briefing more than a living room conversation. Shaniece recounted Dina's revelations while Marcus and David took notes on everything from timeline to threat assessment, their questions revealing minds trained to anticipate dangers that civilian thinking might miss.

"Two million in debt to people who use violence for debt collection," David summarized, his analytical approach complementing Marcus's tactical mindset. "Missing debtor, multiple parties who might be considered viable targets for recovery. Classic case of collateral damage in criminal operations."

Moni shifted uncomfortably in her chair, the clinical language making her friend's danger feel more real and more frightening. "Are we talking about organized crime? Like actual mafia?"

"More likely high-level street operations," Marcus replied. "Organized enough to loan significant money, sophisticated enough to track debtors across state lines, violent enough to make credible threats. The specific organization matters less than their capability and motivation."

As the men discussed tactical considerations, Coko moved closer to Shaniece, their conversation providing counterpoint to strategic planning with spiritual consultation. The relationship between these four friends went deeper than most people realized—bonds forged through three generations of shared history.

"You know our grandmothers would be praying nonstop if they were still with us," Coko observed, her voice carrying the comfort of someone who understood that some friendships transcended individual relationships to become family legacy.

Shaniece nodded, remembering stories of their grandmothers' friendship that had sustained them through everything from the Great Depression to civil rights struggles. Those women had passed down more than recipes and quilting patterns—they'd transmitted understanding that true sisterhood meant showing up regardless of circumstances.

"Mama always said the Lord provides protection through people willing to act," Moni added, watching her husband transform her friend's living room into security headquarters. "I never thought we'd need this kind of protection."

The generational perspective provided comfort that individual friendship couldn't achieve. This wasn't about current crisis—it was the continuation of a support system that had sustained their families through challenges that made current difficulties feel manageable by comparison.

David's voice interrupted their reflection: "We're recommending immediate relocation to a secure facility while we develop a long-term strategy. These people won't give up easily, and your current residence is too exposed for adequate protection."

"I'm not running from my own home," Shaniece replied with conviction that surprised everyone present. "This house represents everything I've built, everything I've fought to achieve. Abandoning it sends the message that criminals can dictate where I live and how I live."

Marcus and David exchanged glances that spoke of military partnerships where communication happened through expression and gesture as much as words. They'd clearly discussed this scenario during their drive to the house.

"Actually," Marcus said carefully, "we have an alternative proposal that might resolve the threat permanently rather than temporarily postponing it."

The shift in atmosphere felt immediate and electric. Moni and Coko leaned forward with expressions mixing curiosity and apprehension, while Shaniece recognized the tone of someone about to suggest something dangerous.

"We create a controlled engagement scenario," David explained, his clinical language failing to disguise the operation's inherent risks. "Use your wealth and social profile to draw these individuals into situations where they reveal themselves, attempt contact or intimidation, and we neutralize the threat through legal channels with law enforcement cooperation."

"You want to use Shaniece as bait," Coko said flatly, her voice carrying the disapproval of someone whose spiritual convictions recoiled from strategies that intentionally courted danger.

"We want to resolve this threat definitively rather than manage it indefinitely," Marcus corrected. "Running and hiding works temporarily, but criminals with two-million-dollar motivation don't typically abandon pursuit. They adapt, wait, find different approaches."

Moni stood abruptly, pacing to the window where moonlight illuminated gardens that had always represented peace and security. "This sounds like something that could get our friend killed. There *has* to be another way—something that doesn't require putting her in harm's way intentionally."

"Every option involves risk," David replied with patience born from years of explaining tactical realities to civilians. "The question is whether we manage that risk proactively or react to threats as they develop naturally."

The philosophical divide between military thinking and civilian caution created tension that filled the room like smoke. One worldview prioritized decisive action to eliminate threats; the other sought protection through avoidance and divine intervention.

"What exactly would this 'controlled engagement' involve?" Shaniece asked, her business mind recognizing the strategic logic even while her survival instincts questioned the wisdom of courting danger.

Marcus pulled out his tablet, revealing surveillance photos and tactical diagrams that transformed abstract discussion into concrete planning. "We stage high-profile events that demonstrates your wealth and accessibility. Something public enough to draw attention but controlled enough for us to monitor every approach."

"Art exhibition," David added with a smile that suggested the idea had already been thoroughly developed. "Private showing of new acquisitions in your home, covered by society magazines, attended by New Orleans elite. Perfect opportunity for criminals to assess targets while providing us multiple advantages for observation and response."

The plan possessed an elegant simplicity that appealed to Shaniece's strategic thinking while terrifying her friends' protective instincts: Creating an irresistible opportunity for criminals to reveal themselves while maintaining tactical advantage through preparation and professional support.

"*Fantaisie* magazine would cover something like that extensively," she mused, her mind already calculating publicity angles and guest lists. "High society loves exclusive access to private collections, especially when they're displayed in homes like this."

"Absolutely not," Moni declared with conviction that made everyone pause. "We are not putting our sister in danger so these men can play soldier. There has to be another way."

"What other way?" Marcus challenged, though his tone remained respectful. "Wait for them to choose a time and place for confrontation? Hope they lose interest or find other targets? Pray that law enforcement can protect her indefinitely without specific threats to investigate?"

The questions hung in the air like incense, heavy with implications that civilian thinking preferred to avoid but military experience couldn't ignore.

Coko moved to stand beside her husband, her internal struggle visible as spousal loyalty warred with protective friendship. "If we do this—and I'm not saying we should—what guarantees do we have that it ends safely?"

"No guarantees," David replied with honesty that cut through comfortable illusions. "But controlled risk beats uncontrolled uncertainty. At least this way, we choose when and where the confrontation happens."

The debate continued for another hour, spiritual principles wrestling with practical necessities while friendship bonds stretched under pressure of protecting someone they all loved. Eventually, Shaniece raised her hand for silence.

"I appreciate everyone's concern, but this is ultimately my decision to make. And I'm thinking about something Jesus said: 'Be wise as serpents and innocent as doves.' Maybe wisdom sometimes means taking calculated risks to protect not just myself, but other potential victims."

She moved to stand beside the window where Dina had appeared hours earlier—desperate young mother fleeing dangers created by the same man whose criminal associations now threatened everyone connected to him.

"If these men are willing to threaten a woman with a newborn baby, they'll threaten other innocent people. Running protects me temporarily but doesn't stop them from finding other targets. Maybe ending this threat permanently is the more loving choice."

Moni and Coko exchanged glances that spoke of friends recognizing familiar determination. When Shaniece made decisions based on spiritual conviction rather than personal comfort, arguing typically proved futile.

"There's biblical precedent," Coko admitted reluctantly. "Esther put herself in danger to protect her people. Rahab risked her life to help God's purposes. Sometimes faith requires courage rather than caution."

"But there's also biblical wisdom about not testing God unnecessarily," Moni countered. "Jumping off the temple to prove divine protection isn't faith—it's presumption."

The theological debate provided a framework for practical decision-making, spiritual principles offering guidance that military training couldn't provide. Faith and tactical planning weren't opposed—they could work together when properly understood.

"Let's move forward with the plan," Shaniece decided, her voice carrying finality that ended discussion. "But we do it with prayer, preparation, and professional support. Divine protection doesn't mean being passive—it means taking wise action while trusting God with the results."

Setting the Trap

The next phase of planning resembled corporate project management more than military operation. Guest lists, catering arrangements, security installations, media coordination—details that would create convincing art exhibition while providing tactical advantages for observation and response.

"I'll need to contact Trange' for the *Fantaisie* connection," Shaniece said, already mentally crafting the conversation that would secure magazine coverage without revealing operational security.

"What do you tell her?" Marcus asked. "How much does she need to know?"

"Nothing about the real purpose. 'Let not your right hand know what your left hand is doing'—biblical principle that applies to operational security as much as spiritual discipline. She gets enough information to help with publicity, nothing more."

The compartmentalization felt uncomfortable given their recent friendship tensions, but wisdom demanded protecting information that could compromise everyone's safety. Trange' would contribute without knowing she was participating in something far more dangerous than a society event.

"Samantha and Margaux need to be fully briefed," Shaniece continued. "If this goes wrong, I'll need legal protection as much as physical security. Plus, Samantha deserves to know what we're doing—she's earned that trust."

Over the next two hours, the men installed surveillance equipment that transformed her home into an observation post, communication systems that connected every room to the central monitoring station, and panic buttons disguised as decorative elements throughout the house.

By dawn, Shaniece's sanctuary had been converted into a carefully constructed trap designed to draw criminals into confrontation they couldn't win. Faith and military expertise working together to create protection through proactive engagement rather than reactive hiding.

Lord, she prayed as the last equipment was installed, I'm trusting that You've provided these protectors for such a time as this. Help us end this threat without anyone getting hurt who doesn't deserve it.

The trap was set. Now they had to wait for predators to take the bait.

CHAPTER 15: DIVINE DELIVERANCE

Autumn evening light filtered through Shaniece's mansion as New Orleans' social elite began arriving for what *Fantaisie* magazine had breathlessly promoted as "the season's most exclusive private art exhibition." Valets parked luxury vehicles in precise rows while guests ascended marble steps dressed in their finest, each one representing either genuine art appreciation or calculated social positioning.

Inside, the transformation was remarkable. Original masterpieces hung at perfect intervals, their museum-quality lighting creating intimate galleries throughout rooms that normally hosted business meetings. Servers in crisp white uniforms circulated with champagne and carefully curated hors d'oeuvres, while a string quartet provided sophisticated background music that elevated conversation without overwhelming it.

Marcus and David moved through the crowd like shadows, their security training disguised beneath perfectly tailored evening wear. To observers, they appeared to be successful businessmen admiring art and networking with New Orleans' power brokers. In reality, they monitored every entrance, catalogued every guest, and maintained constant communication through nearly invisible earpieces.

Trange' had arrived in spectacular form—a flowing emerald Versace gown that commanded attention while she worked the room with social grace that reminded everyone why she was *Fantaisie's* most sought-after correspondent. Her usual sharp edges had softened into charming wit and diplomatic conversation, the persona she adopted when representing the magazine at high-profile events.

"Darling, you've outdone yourself," she gushed to Shaniece, air-kissing both cheeks while photographers captured the moment. "This Monet is absolutely divine, and that Picasso in the corner—where on earth did you find it?"

Shaniece smiled graciously, though her nerves thrummed beneath polished composure. Every new arrival might be the threat they were waiting to expose, every admiring glance at her collection potentially calculated rather than appreciative.

Antoine Bernard Dubois presence announced him to the room before he announced himself by name. Tall and distinguished with silver-touched temples that suggested worldly experience, he moved through the exhibition with confidence that drew attention from multiple directions. His obvious appreciation for the artwork seemed genuine, his questions intelligent and informed.

"Mademoiselle," he said, approaching Trange' with continental charm as she examined a particularly striking abstract piece. "Forgive the intrusion, but your appreciation for this Rothko suggests someone with exceptional artistic sensibility."

Trange' turned with the kind of smile that had launched a thousand magazine features. "Monsieur is too kind. I confess, I find myself completely captivated by the emotional intensity of his color work."

"Ah, a woman who understands that true art speaks to the soul, not merely the intellect." His accent carried hints of French sophistication mixed with something harder to place. "Perhaps you could enlighten me about the provenance of these remarkable pieces? The collection suggests acquisitions from very ... exclusive sources."

Their conversation continued with escalating flirtation, Antoine's compliments becoming more elaborate while Trange' responded with uncharacteristic warmth. The social butterfly persona had emerged, transforming her from sharp-tongued critic into charming conversationalist who seemed genuinely engaged by his attention.

Meanwhile, he'd also spent considerable time studying specific pieces—particularly those positioned near potential exit routes or areas with limited surveillance coverage. When Shaniece approached to welcome him personally, his compliments carried undertones that made her skin crawl despite their superficial politeness.

"Madame Shaw, your reputation for exquisite taste is clearly well-deserved," he said, lifting her hand to his lips in an old-world gesture that felt more invasive than gallant. "Such beauty, such refinement, such ... accessibility. One wonders how someone so lovely could bear to part with even a single treasure."

David materialized beside them, extending his hand in greeting while positioning himself strategically. "Good evening, I'm David Chen. I couldn't help but notice your interest in the pre-Columbian pieces. Are you a collector yourself?"

"Antoine Bernard Dubois," came the reply, though the accent seemed to shift slightly under scrutiny. "I represent certain ... private interests in acquisition and transportation of valuable objects. Perhaps we could discuss mutual opportunities?"

The conversation that followed felt like verbal chess, each man probing the other's knowledge and intentions while maintaining social pleasantries. David's military training detected something predatory beneath Antoine's cultured surface, while

Antoine's responses suggested familiarity with moving valuable items through channels that didn't involve traditional galleries.

The evening's carefully orchestrated atmosphere shattered when Dalvin Shaw appeared in the doorway like a storm cloud blocking out stars. Disheveled, agitated, and clearly under some form of influence, he surveyed the gathering with wild eyes that settled on Shaniece with unmistakable hostility.

"Well, well," his voice carried across the room with a theatrical volume designed to command attention. "Having quite the party with my money, aren't we? All these lovely people admiring art bought with funds stolen from joint accounts?"

Conversations died as guests turned toward the disruption, cameras stopped clicking, and the string quartet faltered into silence. Shaniece felt blood drain from her face as months of careful reputation rebuilding threatened to crumble under public accusation.

Marcus moved immediately, intercepting Dalvin before he could advance further into the room. "Sir, this is a private event. I'm going to have to ask you to leave."

"Private? Nothing's private when it's bought with embezzled money!" Dalvin's voice rose to near-shouting. "Ask my dear wife how she funded this little art collection. Ask her about the joint investments she liquidated without permission!"

Samantha appeared from across the room like an avenging angel, her burgundy dress streaming behind her as she prepared to physically remove the man who dared disrupt her sister's evening. But David blocked her path with subtle but firm intervention.

"Ma'am, we've got this under control," he murmured, though his positioning suggested readiness for multiple contingencies.

The confrontation escalated when Dalvin attempted to push past Marcus, his coordination impaired but his anger amplified by whatever substances coursed through his system. "You have no right to keep me from my own house! From my own wife!"

"Your former house," Marcus corrected. "Your former wife. And you have exactly thirty seconds to leave voluntarily before we assist your departure."

What happened next felt choreographed despite its apparent spontaneity. Dalvin's protests grew louder, drawing security and guests toward the front entrance, when suddenly the mansion plunged into complete darkness. Emergency lighting failed to activate, backup systems remained silent, and the sophisticated surveillance network went blind.

In the chaos that followed, Marcus and David immediately shifted into tactical mode, their voices cutting through confused conversations with authority that brooked no argument.

"Ladies and gentlemen, we're experiencing technical difficulties," David announced into the darkness. "For everyone's safety, we're going to need you to exit through the front entrance in an orderly fashion. Staff will guide you to your vehicles."

"This is just a precaution," Marcus added, though his hand had moved instinctively toward the concealed weapon beneath his jacket. "Thank you for your cooperation and understanding."

The evacuation proceeded with remarkable efficiency, guests filing out with disappointed murmurs about the evening's premature conclusion. Trange' had started to leave with the others but returned for a charcuterie board she'd specifically requested from the caterers.

"I'm not wasting that imported brie," she declared to Shaniece with characteristic determination. "You go rest. I'll lock up when I leave."

Within twenty minutes, the mansion stood empty except for Shaniece and Trange', while outside, Marcus and David conducted security sweeps with frustrated accuracy. Their carefully planned trap had failed spectacularly—no suspects apprehended, no threats neutralized, nothing accomplished except disruption of an expensive evening.

Power restored itself as mysteriously as it had failed, surveillance cameras blinking back to life while normal lighting returned throughout the mansion. Marcus and David conducted thorough sweeps to ensure all artwork remained secure and no uninvited guests had remained behind during the confusion.

"I don't understand it," Marcus admitted as they prepared to depart. "The backup generators should have activated automatically. The surveillance system has triple redundancy. None of this makes technical sense."

"Maybe it was a coincidence," Shaniece suggested, though doubt colored her voice. "Old houses, electrical problems, bad timing."

"Military training teaches us not to believe in coincidences," David replied grimly. "But we've verified everything is secure. All artwork accounted for, all entry points checked, all systems operational."

They packed their equipment with visible frustration, another security consultation that had failed to produce results. Moni and Coko offered comfort to their friend while their husbands loaded surveillance gear into black SUVs that would return them to lives where threats could be clearly identified and decisively addressed.

"Thank you for everything," Shaniece said as they prepared to leave. "I know this didn't work out as planned, but I feel safer knowing you were here."

"We'll continue monitoring the situation," Marcus promised. "And we'll be reviewing tonight's events to understand what went wrong."

As the vehicles disappeared down her circular driveway, Shaniece watched from her front door until taillights vanished beyond the gates. Exhaustion settled over her like fog, the combination of social performance and underlying tension finally taking its toll.

Upstairs in her master bedroom, Shaniece finally allowed herself to relax. The evening had been a disaster from an operational standpoint, but perhaps that was divine intervention preventing a confrontation that could have turned violent. Sometimes failed plans served purposes beyond human understanding.

She slipped into silk pajamas and settled into her four-poster bed, pulling on the sleep mask that blocked out ambient light and helped her achieve the deep rest that executive responsibilities demanded. Tomorrow would bring new challenges, but tonight, she was simply grateful to be safe in her own home.

Downstairs, Trange' surveyed the dining room with satisfaction, locating the specific charcuterie board whose imported cheeses had captured her attention earlier in the evening. She'd driven herself tonight, wanting the freedom to leave when social obligations were satisfied rather than waiting for shared transportation.

The power failure struck again without warning, plunging the mansion into darkness so complete that her breath caught in her throat. She fumbled for her phone, its screen providing the only illumination as she tried to navigate familiar rooms that felt alien in absolute blackness.

Her phone began ringing, the sound echoing through empty spaces while its light guided her movement. She started toward the source when a soft creak near the wall made her freeze. The sound had come from inside the room, not from the hallways or upper floors.

A figure emerged from what had appeared to be a solid wall, moving with practiced silence toward her position. She opened her mouth to scream but a hand clamped over her lips while an arm circled her waist, lifting her feet from the floor as she struggled against professional restraint.

The antique vase she knocked over shattered against marble with crystal clarity, its destruction marking the moment when elegant evening transformed into something far more sinister. Additional figures materialized from the same hidden entrance, their coordination suggesting military training adapted for criminal purposes.

Racing Against Time

Miles away, Marcus was explaining the evening's failure to David when Coko's casual observation stopped their conversation cold.

"You know what was really odd? The power going out when there's a backup generator. These old Garden District houses always have generators—they were built for people who couldn't afford to lose electricity during hurricane season."

Moni nodded from the passenger seat. "Plus Dalvin showing up like that, right when everything went wrong. The timing was almost too perfect."

David's analytical mind began processing implications he'd missed during the crisis. "You're right. The generators should have activated automatically. And Dalvin's disruption provided perfect cover for whatever caused the blackout."

"But there was nothing to steal," Marcus pointed out. "We checked every piece. Everything was exactly where it should be."

"Maybe theft wasn't the goal," Coko mused. "Maybe the disruption was the goal. Draw attention away from something else."

"But what else could they want?" Moni asked, then paused as understanding began dawning. "Oh God. Dalvin would know the house layout. He'd know about the servants' passages."

"The what?" both men asked simultaneously.

"The hidden entrances," Coko explained, her voice rising with growing alarm. "All these antebellum houses have them—passages that allowed servants to move through the house without disrupting formal gatherings. Dalvin showed them to me years ago. They connect to the wine cellar, the kitchen, even some of the upstairs bedrooms."

Marcus slammed the brakes so hard that tires screamed against asphalt. The realization hit like a physical impact: Dalvin's scene had forced them to evacuate everyone, the power failure had disabled their surveillance, and in the confusion, someone could have remained hidden in passages they'd never thought to check.

"Call Shaniece," David ordered, already pulling his weapon while Marcus executed a sharp U-turn. "Call Trange'. Get them both on the phone now."

Moni's fingers flew across her phone screen while her heart hammered against her ribs. Shaniece's line went straight to voicemail. Trange's phone rang endlessly without answer.

"Floor it," David commanded, chambering a round as their SUV raced back toward the Garden District. "And call for backup. This isn't a failed security consultation anymore—this is a rescue operation."

Behind them, city lights blurred past like streaking stars while two military-trained professionals prepared for the kind of operation they'd hoped would never be necessary. Time had become their enemy, distance their obstacle, and somewhere in the darkness ahead, their friends needed help that might already be arriving too late.

CHAPTER 16: THE FINAL GAMBIT

The Trap Revealed

Trange' struggled against the rope binding her to the antique dining chair, her emerald Versace gown torn at the shoulder where rough hands had grabbed her. Five masked figures moved through Shaniece's living room, lifting priceless artwork from walls with practiced efficiency. Her muffled screams echoed through rooms that had hosted elegant conversation just hours earlier.

"Shaniece!" she tried to yell through the tape covering her mouth, desperate to warn her friend of the invasion happening beneath her bedroom. But only strangled sounds emerged as panic clawed at her throat.

The tallest figure approached her with predatory confidence, pulling away his mask to reveal the sophisticated features of Antoine Bernard Dubois. His cultured accent dissolved into crude American English as transformation completed itself.

"Save your breath, beautiful," he sneered, his earlier continental charm replaced by street-hardened malice. "Your friend can't hear you anyway. We slipped something special in her tea when she went upstairs. She'll be dreaming sweet dreams for hours."

His laughter carried the satisfaction of someone whose elaborate plan was unfolding exactly as designed. With casual cruelty, he ripped the tape from her mouth, taking pleasure in her sharp intake of breath.

"You're going to pay for this!" Trange' demanded, though her voice trembled with fear she couldn't suppress.

Antoine leaned close enough that she could smell cigarettes and something chemical on his breath. "Pay? Who's gonna make me pay, princess?"

He produced a switchblade with theatrical flourish, the steel catching light from the crystal chandelier as he traced it along her cheek with surgeon's precision. "Don't tempt me to take this back to the old ways. I'd love to hear you scream and beg like the others."

Lord, if You're there, I need You now, Trange' prayed silently, her earlier skepticism about divine intervention crumbling under immediate terror. *I don't want to die like this.*

The Heist Unfolds

Terror crystallized into sharp clarity as Trange' surveyed her surroundings, searching desperately for any possibility of escape or rescue. Through doorways leading to other rooms, she glimpsed more masked figures emerging from hidden passages she'd never known existed, carrying paintings and sculptures worth millions.

The systematic efficiency was chilling—they knew exactly which pieces held the greatest value, where security cameras were positioned, how to move through the house without triggering alarms that should have activated automatically.

"Monsieur Dubois, we have what we need," called one of the figures emerging from a concealed doorway near the kitchen. "Time to go."

Antoine straightened, his knife still dancing dangerously close to her throat. "Almost finished here, Derek," he replied, his accent shifting again as he spoke to his accomplice.

He noticed the abandoned charcuterie board on the side table, its imported cheeses and artisanal crackers a grotesque reminder of the evening's earlier elegance. With mockery that felt more threatening than his blade, he prepared a small portion and held it toward her lips.

"A token of my affection, ma chérie," he whispered with a renewed fake accent. "For the lovely evening you provided."

But as he looked into her eyes, expecting to see only terror, something else flickered in her gaze. For just a moment, beneath the fear, he glimpsed something harder—calculation, defiance, perhaps even anticipation.

The expression confused him enough that he stepped backward, momentarily uncertain.

That's when he heard the distinctive click of a weapon being cocked behind his head.

"Make one move and we'll be redecorating these walls with your brain matter," Marcus commanded, his voice carrying deadly calm as cold steel pressed against Antoine's skull. "Drop the knife. Now."

The blade clattered against marble with sound like breaking crystal, its threat neutralized by military training that had anticipated exactly this scenario. Through the secret passage that had allowed criminals entry, David emerged with zip-ties securing two additional suspects.

"Target secured," David reported with systematic efficiency. "We've got three more bundled up like Christmas presents in the wine cellar."

Moni and Coko appeared through the same hidden entrance, their faces mixing shock with unmistakable pride in their husbands' professional competence. The women who'd worried about putting their friend in danger now witnessed the surgical efficiency that made that protection possible.

"Where's Shaniece?" Coko asked urgently, already moving toward the stairs.

"Upstairs," Trange' managed, her voice hoarse from suppressed screams. "They drugged her tea. She needs help."

As Coko rushed to check on their friend, Moni and Marcus worked to free Trange' from her restraints. The rope had cut into her wrists, leaving marks that would serve as evidence of the night's violence.

David surveyed the crime scene with professional assessment. "This was sophisticated. They almost outmaneuvered us completely. We're getting old, partner."

Marcus secured handcuffs on Antoine with satisfaction that bordered on vindictiveness. "I thought you were going to get away with this elaborate scheme. Almost brilliant, if you hadn't underestimated military intelligence."

Antoine hung his head in defeat, his earlier arrogance evaporating under the weight of capture and inevitable prosecution.

"Don't get quiet on us now," David taunted. "The police are on their way, and they'll have plenty of questions about your little art theft operation."

Sirens wailed in the distance, growing closer with each passing second.

Freedom from restraints unleashed emotions Trange' had been forced to suppress during her captivity. She stalked toward Antoine with fury that had been building since the moment his hands first touched her.

"Don't you ever lay hands on a woman again!" she shouted, her palm connecting with his cheek in sharp slaps that echoed through the room. "You pathetic excuse for a man!"

David moved quickly to restrain her before vigilante justice could escalate beyond therapeutic necessity. "Save some fight for the courtroom testimony. The police will need you to be coherent."

But her anger felt righteous, defensible, even biblical—the fury of someone who'd faced evil and survived to see justice served through divine timing and human courage working together.

Upstairs, Coko's voice carried panic that cut through the house like a blade through silk. "We need an ambulance! Something's wrong with Shaniece!"

She'd found her friend motionless on the bed, breathing so shallowly it was barely detectable. No amount of shaking or calling her name produced any response—the elegant woman who'd hosted the evening's gathering lay still as death.

Moni rushed upstairs to help while the men below processed the implications of what they were hearing. Marcus turned to Antoine with expression that could have melted steel.

"What did you give her?"

"Just a mild sedative," Antoine replied with casual indifference that inflamed rather than calmed the situation. "Nothing that should—"

"A sedative with alcohol can kill someone, you idiot!" David interrupted, his medical training from military service recognizing the potentially lethal combination.

The realization hit Antoine like a physical blow, his face cycling through emotions as he calculated whether he'd committed art theft or manslaughter. Marcus seized him by the shirt, slamming him against the wall with force that rattled picture frames.

"I swear on everything holy, if something happens to her, I'm coming for you personally," Marcus growled, his military restraint finally cracking under protective fury.

Antoine's response was hysterical laughter that echoed through the mansion like a demonic chorus, drowning out the prayers and crying from upstairs where two women fought to keep their friend conscious until medical help arrived.

Police sirens screamed onto the property as emergency medical technicians rushed through the front door with equipment that might save a life hanging in the balance. The elegant mansion had become a crime scene and medical emergency.

Upstairs, paramedics worked with professional efficiency to stabilize Shaniece while Moni and Coko prayed with desperation borne of watching someone they loved slip away before their eyes.

"Lord, please don't take her," Coko whispered, her hands clasped so tightly her knuckles were white. "She's got so much more to give, so many people who need her strength."

"We need You to fight for her when she can't fight for herself," Moni added, tears streaming down her cheeks as medical professionals prepared their friend for transport.

The paramedics found a pulse—weak but steady—and immediately began IV fluids to flush the dangerous combination from her system. Within minutes, they had her strapped to a gurney and were racing toward the hospital where emergency physicians would determine whether divine intervention and medical science could collaborate to save her life.

As the ambulance disappeared into the night, Trange' surveyed the wreckage of what had been an elegant evening. Artwork scattered across floors, furniture overturned, police tape marking areas where her ordeal had unfolded. The magnitude of destruction—physical, emotional, spiritual—felt overwhelming.

She approached Marcus and David with tear-streaked determination that commanded their attention despite the chaos surrounding them.

"Something more happened here tonight," she declared, her voice carrying authority that refused deflection. "You both know things you haven't told me. I want the truth. Now."

The military men exchanged glances that spoke of classified information and operational security, but Trange's experience had earned her the right to complete honesty.

"My friend is in the hospital fighting for her life. I was tied to a chair and threatened with death. Some psychopath pretended to be French while planning to kill me after robbing millions in artwork. You're going to tell me *everything*!"

With their wives gone and their friend's life hanging in the balance, Marcus and David recognized that half-truths would no longer suffice. The woman who'd survived tonight's ordeal deserved to understand exactly what forces had been arrayed against them all.

"Where do we start?" David asked, knowing that full disclosure would shatter whatever illusions remained about the sophisticated criminal operation they'd barely managed to defeat.

Trange' wiped tears from her cheeks with hands that still bore rope burns from her captivity. "Start at the *beginning*. I want to know *everything* about why someone just tried to kill me over stolen art."

Lord, she prayed silently as she prepared for revelations that would change her understanding of everything that had transpired, *help me be strong enough to handle whatever truth they're about to tell me.*

CHAPTER 17: NEW BEGINNINGS

***

The Master's Confession

Dalvin's voice carried the satisfaction of someone whose elaborate scheme had unfolded exactly as planned, each word recorded by the device that would ultimately destroy him. From her hospital bed, Shaniece lay motionless, eyes closed, controlling her breathing while her ex-husband revealed the full scope of his betrayal to whoever was listening on the other end of his call.

"Let me walk you through the genius of this operation," he continued, pacing near the window with arrogance that made her stomach turn. "First, I cultivated the relationship with Antoine and his crew months ago. Told them about the art collection, the house layout, even drew them floor plans of those secret passages nobody else knew about."

Lord, give me strength to hear this without breaking, she prayed silently, fighting the urge to open her eyes and confront the monster who'd once promised to love and protect her.

"The security consultation was perfect," Dalvin laughed with genuine amusement. "Those military boys thought they were so smart, installing their cameras and motion detectors. But they never knew about the servants' passages, did they? Antoine and his team hid in there during the power outage, then emerged later to grab the artwork while everyone was evacuating."

He paused, listening to his accomplice, then chuckled again. "Oh, the power? I had my boy Jimmy cut the main lines right before the chaos started. Disabled their precious surveillance system and backup generators in one move. Military training doesn't help when you don't know the playing field, bruh."

Tears threatened to break through her closed eyelids as she realized how thoroughly he'd manipulated everyone who'd tried to protect her. David and Marcus had risked their lives based on incomplete information.

"Trange' was an unexpected element," he admitted with casual cruelty. "She wasn't supposed to stay behind for that ridiculous cheese board. But it worked out beautifully—gave Antoine's crew more time to work, and now she can testify about the 'random break-in' that nearly killed my poor wife."

The recording device captured every word as he revealed the depths of his premeditation.

"The sedative was my personal touch," his voice carried pride in his own cleverness. "I've been watching her routine for weeks. Every night at precisely 10:30, she makes herself that Meyer lemon tea. A bit of, honey, a slice of fresh lemon—same ritual every single night. All I had to do was slip in during the party chaos and add a little something extra to her tea blend."

He was in my house, she realized with horror. During the exhibition, while I was entertaining guests, he snuck upstairs and poisoned my tea.

"I didn't expect the allergic reaction," Dalvin continued, "but honestly, it's better than I could have planned. Makes the whole thing look completely accidental. Who's going to suspect that someone deliberately triggered a medical emergency during a robbery?"

He moved closer to her bed, and she fought to keep her breathing steady as his shadow fell across her face.

"The beauty of it all is the timing," he explained to his listener. "Get the artwork to pay off my gambling debts, collect the two million life insurance payout, and inherit everything else through spousal rights. By this time next month, I'll be debt-free with millions to spare. Might even take a nice vacation to celebrate my recovery from grief."

Father, I know You told me to forgive, but this level of evil tests every principle You've taught me, she prayed, struggling to maintain her façade of unconsciousness while recording evidence that would ensure justice.

The medical team entered her room with solemn efficiency, their presence transforming the space from recovery area into legal battlefield. Dr. Harper carried paperwork that would authorize the termination of life support—documents that represented the difference between life and death for someone fighting to survive.

"Mr. Shaw," Dr. Harper said carefully, her voice carrying professional reluctance. "These are the authorization forms for discontinuing artificial life support. I have to advise you that your wife's condition has stabilized, and there's still hope for recovery."

"Doctor, I appreciate your medical opinion," Dalvin replied with false compassion that fooled no one except potentially a jury. "But I know my wife better than anyone. She wouldn't want to exist as a vegetable, connected to machines. The merciful thing is to let her go peacefully."

Through the doorway, Shaniece could hear Moni and Samantha pleading with nurses to let them enter, their voices carrying desperation of people watching someone they loved being systematically murdered by bureaucratic procedure.

"Please," Samantha's voice cracked with emotion. "Let us say goodbye. Let us pray with her. Don't let him make this decision without family present."

"I'm sorry," came the nurse's response, "but only the spouse has legal authority in this situation."

Dalvin signed the documents with a flourish that suggested satisfaction rather than sorrow, each signature bringing him closer to wealth built on the foundation of his wife's death.

"How long?" he asked with clinical interest that revealed his true priorities.

"Once we remove the breathing assistance, it could be minutes or hours," Dr. Harper replied reluctantly. "There's no way to predict exactly."

"I understand," Dalvin nodded with mock solemnity. "I'll need time to grieve privately after … after she's gone. Please ensure I'm not disturbed."

The medical team began approaching her bed with equipment that would end her life, their professional duty overriding personal instincts that something felt wrong about the entire situation.

As hands reached toward the machines keeping her alive, Shaniece opened her eyes with dramatic timing that would have impressed Hollywood directors. The sudden movement froze everyone in place—medical staff stepping backward, Dalvin's face cycling through shock and rage, and voices from the hallway erupting in praise.

"Praise the Lord!" Coko's voice carried through the doorway with power that made nurses stop their procedures. "She's awake! God has brought her back!"

"Thank You, Jesus!" Moni added, her prayer carrying the authority of someone who'd witnessed a genuine miracle. "We knew You wouldn't take her yet!"

Dalvin's expression transformed from mock sorrow to undisguised fury as his carefully orchestrated plan crumbled before his eyes. The woman who was supposed to die quietly had awakened at the precise moment that would expose his true nature to medical professionals and potential witnesses. They rushed to remove her intubation as Shanice tried to remove it herself. Once removed, she struggled to breathe but quickly regained her composure.

"Hello, everyone," Shaniece said softly, her voice carrying strength that belied hours of medical crisis. She turned toward the doorway where her friends waited, her eyes finding Samantha's tear-streaked face. "You can't get rid of me that easily."

Her smile carried peace that earthly circumstances couldn't disturb—evidence of divine encounters that had strengthened her for battles yet to come.

In the chaos of celebration and medical reassessment, Margaux Morrison arrived like reinforcement cavalry, her presence transforming the room from medical crisis to legal battlefield. Her silver hair caught fluorescent light as she surveyed the situation with tactical precision that matched her courtroom reputation.

"What's the current status?" she asked Dr. Harper with authority that commanded immediate response.

"The patient has regained consciousness and appears stable," the doctor replied, relief evident in her voice. "The authorization to discontinue life support is now medically appropriate."

As friends gathered around her bed offering prayers and praise for her recovery, Shaniece caught Samantha's attention with subtle gesture that conveyed urgent communication needed. When her dearest friend leaned close for what appeared to be an emotional embrace, Shaniece slipped her phone into Samantha's hands with whispered instructions that would change everything.

"Listen to the recording with Margaux," she murmured against Samantha's ear. "Do whatever you can legally to protect me. The truth is all there."

Samantha's eyes widened as she recognized the implications, her grip tightening on the device that contained evidence of conspiracy, attempted murder, and insurance fraud that would destroy Dalvin more thoroughly than any revenge they could have planned.

"I need to secure her medical care," Samantha announced with executive authority. "Dr. Harper, I want her moved to a private room immediately. And I need you to restrict access to only the people on this list." She began writing names with precision that excluded certain individuals while including others.

"Additionally," she continued, turning to Marcus and David who'd arrived with their wives, "I need you to secure her house as a crime scene and post security outside this room. We're done playing defense. It's time for offense."

She grabbed Margaux's arm with determination that brooked no argument. "We need to talk. Privately. Now."

As they departed to review evidence that would reshape the entire legal landscape, Dalvin stood frozen in the corner, his rage barely contained as he watched his perfect plan disintegrate in real time and slithered out of the room.

Sacred Moments

Alone with Moni and Coko after the exodus of legal and security personnel, Shaniece felt peace settle over the room like divine presence making itself known. The women who'd prayed for her recovery now ministered with oil and words that carried power beyond medical intervention.

"Father, we thank You for bringing our sister back from the valley of the shadow of death," Moni prayed, anointing Shaniece's forehead with oil that carried blessing beyond its physical properties. "We know You have purposes for her life that enemy schemes cannot destroy."

"Grant her wisdom for the battles ahead," Coko added, her voice resonant with authority that came from witnessing genuine miracles. "Help her walk in Your ways as justice unfolds according to Your perfect timing."

After her friends departed, Shaniece turned toward the window where sunset painted the sky in shades of gold and crimson. The day that had begun with an elegant art exhibition and ended with attempted murder was finally concluding but tomorrow would bring opportunities for justice that human wisdom couldn't orchestrate alone.

Lord, she prayed as darkness settled over New Orleans, You've brought me through the valley and shown me Your purposes. Now give me wisdom to end this situation in ways that honor You while protecting others from the evil that almost destroyed me.

As she drifted toward healing sleep, divine vision filled her mind—clear understanding of how justice and mercy would work together to transform Dalvin's evil into an instrument of ultimate good. She rested knowing that tomorrow would bring battles but also knowing Who held both today and tomorrow in hands that were powerful enough to defeat any enemy while gentle enough to heal every wound.

A soft knock interrupted her prayers as Dr. Harper entered with clipboard and expression that mixed relief with something approaching wonder.

"Mrs. Shaw, I wanted to update you on your test results before you rest," she said, settling into the bedside chair with careful professionalism. "The toxicology reports show that the sedative is completely out of your system. Your liver and kidney functions are normal, and there appears to be no lasting damage from the allergic reaction."

"Thank God," Shaniece whispered, tears of gratitude flowing freely. "I was so afraid there might be permanent effects."

"You should know," Dr. Harper continued with a smile that suggested she was about to deliver unexpected news, "both you and the baby appear to be completely unaffected by the ordeal."

Shaniece sat upright so quickly that monitors began beeping alarm warnings. "A baby? What baby?"

Dr. Harper's expression shifted to surprise. "You didn't know? Based on the ultrasound scans we performed during your treatment, you're approximately eight weeks pregnant. I assumed you were aware of your condition."

The room seemed to spin as implications crashed over her like tidal waves. "Doctor, that's impossible. I'm infertile. I haven't been able to conceive for years due to ... complications from when I was younger."

"Well, your ovaries apparently think differently," Dr. Harper replied with gentle humor. "And God moves in mysterious ways. The pregnancy is perfectly healthy, and the baby's heartbeat is strong. You're fighting for two now."

Shaniece's hand moved instinctively to her abdomen, where new life grew despite every medical prediction to the contrary. The irony wasn't lost on her—while Dalvin plotted her death for financial gain, divine life was creating itself within her body.

"Dr. Harper," she whispered urgently, gripping the physician's hand, "please don't tell anyone about this yet. With everything that's happening legally, I need time to process this news and decide how to handle it safely."

"Of course," the doctor replied with understanding that went beyond professional duty. "Patient confidentiality absolutely applies. I'll have the OB-GYN see you tomorrow for proper prenatal care, but your secret is safe with me."

"Thank you," Shaniece breathed, overwhelmed by the magnitude of divine intervention that had not only saved her life but granted her the impossible gift she'd mourned for years.

As Dr. Harper departed, Shaniece lay back against her pillows with hand resting protectively over the miracle growing within her. The recording on Samantha's phone would ensure earthly justice, but the peace in her heart promised something far greater—new life that represented hope, redemption, and God's ability to create beauty from even the darkest circumstances.

Lord, she prayed through tears of joy and amazement, You've not only brought me through the valley but given me reason to fight for the future. Help me protect this precious gift while justice unfolds according to Your perfect plan.

Tomorrow would bring battles with Dalvin's legal team, but tonight she rested knowing that she carried within her body the ultimate victory over his schemes—life that he could never destroy, hope that his hatred could never extinguish, and promise that God's purposes would prevail regardless of human evil.

CHAPTER 18: HEALING THE SISTERHOOD

Reflections and Revelations

One month after the ordeal that had nearly claimed her life, Shaniece stood before her bedroom mirror examining the subtle changes that marked new life growing within her. The slight curve of her abdomen was barely visible beneath her flowing silk blouse, but to her it represented a miracle beyond medical explanation.

The timing of conception had become clear through careful calculation—that vulnerable night when Dalvin had returned to collect his remaining belongings, playing the remorseful husband seeking reconciliation. She'd weakened momentarily, allowing loneliness and hope to override wisdom that should have protected her heart. That same evening, he'd likely observed her nightly tea ritual, gathering intelligence for the murder plot that would unfold weeks later.

The irony is breathtaking, she reflected, her hand moving protectively over the small bump. While he was plotting to destroy my life, God was creating new life within me. Even in my moment of weakness, divine purpose was at work.

The past month had brought necessary solitude for processing trauma and preparing for battles ahead. Samantha had assumed operational control of Hermosa with characteristic efficiency, protecting the business empire while her friend focused on healing and legal warfare. Trange' had checked in periodically—tentative gestures that suggested desire for reconciliation without willingness to abandon her philosophical positions.

Renee had become equally reclusive, her bitterness over her own divorce creating walls that friendship couldn't easily penetrate. Only Moni and Coko maintained regular contact, their marriages to the men who'd saved her life creating bonds stronger than philosophical differences.

Once this situation with Dalvin reaches resolution, I'll need to address our fractured sisterhood, she thought, recognizing that some relationships might be beyond repair while others required intentional restoration.

But today demanded focus on immediate threats rather than future friendships.

Margaux Morrison had worked with an intensity that bordered on obsession during the weeks following Dalvin's exposure. The silver-haired attorney had coordinated with the District Attorney's office, filed emergency motions for divorce finalization, and gathered evidence that would ensure Dalvin Shaw faced consequences proportionate to his crimes.

"The recording you captured provides overwhelming evidence of conspiracy, attempted murder, and insurance fraud," Margaux had explained during their strategy session. "Combined with testimony from the criminals he hired, we have enough evidence to ensure he never threatens you again."

The coordination between civil and criminal proceedings required precision timing that would eliminate any possibility of

Dalvin escaping justice through legal technicalities or procedural delays. Today's confrontation would determine whether months of careful preparation would achieve the decisive victory that safety required.

As Shaniece prepared for the meeting that would reshape her future, she made the final decision about when to reveal her pregnancy. The secret would remain hers until after the divorce was finalized and Dalvin was safely behind bars where his manipulation could no longer endanger her or their unborn child.

The Confrontation Chamber

The law offices of Dalvin's attorney occupied the fifteenth floor of a glass tower in New Orleans' business district, its conference room designed to intimidate through architectural grandeur rather than comfort. Floor-to-ceiling windows offered commanding views of the Mississippi River while mahogany paneling and oil paintings of legal luminaries created an atmosphere of institutional authority that had witnessed countless professional destructions.

Dalvin sat beside his attorney with arrogance that suggested he expected this meeting to proceed according to his preferences. His expensive suit and carefully groomed appearance projected the confidence of someone who believed wealth and cunning could overcome any legal challenge. The smirk playing around his lips indicated anticipation of watching his ex-wife's legal team struggle against superior strategy.

When the massive conference room doors opened, he straightened in his chair expecting to see the parade of attorneys and advisors that complex legal battles typically required. Instead, three figures entered with purpose that immediately shifted the room's energy.

Shaniece moved first, her burgundy Donna Karan blazer and matching pencil skirt creating a silhouette that commanded respect while suggesting someone prepared for warfare. Her hair swept into an elegant chignon revealed features that carried peace despite the circumstances—evidence of spiritual strength that earthly battles couldn't disturb.

Margaux followed with silver hair catching light from crystal chandeliers, her presence transforming the space from corporate meeting to tribunal where justice would be administered with surgical precision. Her briefcase struck the polished table with sound like gavel announcing verdicts.

The third figure—a uniformed police officer whose stern bearing and hand resting near his service weapon—created an atmosphere of law enforcement rather than civil negotiation. His presence suggested that today's proceedings might conclude with handcuffs rather than handshakes.

"Good morning, gentlemen," Margaux announced with a voice that could cut diamonds. "Shall we proceed with the dissolution of this marriage?"

Dalvin's attorney cleared his throat with practiced authority. "Mrs. Morrison, my client is prepared to negotiate reasonable terms for asset division and spousal support. Mr. Shaw has significant claims to marital property and—"

"I'm afraid you've misunderstood the purpose of this meeting," Margaux interrupted with a smile that carried no warmth. "Mrs. Shaw walks away with everything. Mr. Shaw walks away with nothing except his freedom, and even that may be temporary."

The pronouncement hit the room like physical force. Dalvin shot upright in his chair, his carefully maintained composure cracking to reveal rage beneath expensive clothing.

"That's ridiculous!" he declared, voice rising beyond professional decorum. "I have legal rights! Community property laws! She can't just—"

"Mr. Shaw," Margaux commanded with authority that made him freeze mid-sentence, "I suggest you sit down and listen carefully. Officer Martinez is here for our protection, and his purpose will become clear momentarily."

Curiosity flickered across Dalvin's features before arrogance reasserted itself. The presence of law enforcement seemed more theatrical than threatening to someone convinced of his own cleverness.

"Furthermore," Margaux continued, spreading documents across the mahogany surface, "my client will be reverting to her maiden name. You will no longer have any connection to the Mfume family or its business interests."

Dalvin scoffed with disdain that filled the conference room. "Based on what grounds? Irreconcilable differences? Please. I'll contest every—"

"Based on criminal grounds," Margaux replied with finality that silenced his protests. "Which brings us to the real purpose of today's meeting."

She gestured toward Officer Martinez, who stepped outside briefly before returning with a woman whose presence immediately elevated the proceedings from civil dispute to criminal prosecution.

The woman who entered commanded attention through professional bearing rather than physical intimidation. ADA Sharon Masters-McGee possessed the kind of quiet authority that came from years of prosecuting complex criminal cases in Louisiana's most challenging jurisdiction. Her charcoal gray suit and auburn hair pulled into a simple style suggested someone more concerned with results than appearances.

"Gentlemen," she announced, settling into a chair with efficiency that brooked no argument about her authority, "I'm Assistant District Attorney Sharon Masters-McGee. I've reviewed extensive evidence regarding Mr. Shaw's recent activities, and I'm here to formally charge him with multiple felonies."

The transformation in the room's atmosphere was immediate and electric. Dalvin's face cycled through confusion, recognition, and growing panic as implications became clear.

"Additionally," ADA Masters-McGee continued, "I'd like to introduce Chief Detective Howard, who has been coordinating this investigation from the beginning."

Officer Martinez straightened as his true identity was revealed—not mere security, but a senior law enforcement official who'd been gathering evidence throughout the meeting.

"Mr. Shaw," ADA Masters-McGee began with clinical precision, "you are hereby charged with conspiracy to commit murder, attempted murder, insurance fraud, criminal conspiracy, and aggravated assault. The evidence against you includes recorded confessions, testimony from co-conspirators, physical evidence, and financial records documenting your crimes."

The charges hung in the air like judgment day pronouncements. Dalvin's attorney leaned forward desperately.

"This is highly irregular! We demand to see evidence! Our client maintains his innocence and—"

"Your client confessed to these crimes on a recorded phone call while his victim lay unconscious in a hospital bed," ADA Masters-McGee replied with devastating calm. "He detailed his conspiracy with known criminals, admitted to poisoning his wife, and discussed plans to collect life insurance from her death. Would you like to hear the recording?"

Dalvin erupted from his chair with violence that prompted Chief Howard to reach for his weapon, the movement freezing everyone in place with recognition that civilization hung by threads thinner than anyone had imagined.

"This is impossible!" Dalvin shouted, his face flushed red with rage that revealed the monster beneath expensive suits. "You can't prove any of this! I'll fight these charges! I'll—"

"Mr. Shaw," Chief Howard commanded with authority that filled the room, "I suggest you sit down and compose yourself before this situation escalates beyond civil discourse."

The implied threat achieved immediate compliance. Dalvin slumped back into his chair, his lawyer frantically shuffling through papers while calculating the impossibility of defending against recorded confessions.

"Due to the severity of these charges and Mr. Shaw's access to significant financial resources," ADA Masters-McGee continued, "he will be taken into custody immediately without possibility of bail pending trial."

As handcuffs clicked around Dalvin's wrists with metallic finality, Margaux delivered the final legal blow that would complete his destruction.

"Furthermore," she announced with satisfaction that years of preparation had earned, "due to these criminal charges, Mr. Shaw's consent for divorce dissolution is no longer required. This case will go before a judge immediately, and the marriage will be dissolved by emergency order within twenty-four hours."

Watching her husband—soon to be ex-husband—processed into the criminal justice system, Shaniece felt emotions too complex for simple categorization. Part of her rejoiced that justice was finally served, but another part mourned the man she'd once loved who'd chosen evil over redemption.

Her hand moved instinctively to her abdomen where new life grew, carrying Dalvin's DNA but representing hope rather than his corruption. The secret would remain hers until after legal proceedings concluded and he was safely contained where his manipulation could harm no one.

Lord, she prayed silently, help me protect this precious life while justice unfolds. Help me forgive even as consequences are administered.

As they prepared to escort Dalvin from the building, Margaux rose with theatrical flair that suggested she'd been waiting for this moment throughout her entire legal career.

"Mr. Shaw," she called out as handcuffs secured his hands behind his back, "before you depart, I wanted to reintroduce you to the new Shaniece Amari Mfume. She's reclaiming her family name and her life, neither of which you'll ever touch again."

The words carried finality that marked not just the end of marriage but the beginning of genuine freedom. Shaniece smiled, recognizing that today marked rebirth in every sense—new name, new life growing within her, new future unlimited by past mistakes.

In the corridor outside the conference room, Samantha and Trange' waited with expressions mixing anticipation and protective fury. When Dalvin emerged in handcuffs flanked by law enforcement, the confrontation that followed would have been comedic if not for its underlying seriousness.

"Bye, boo," Samantha called out with theatrical sweetness, blowing a kiss that dripped with sarcasm. "Don't worry—we'll take good care of everything you're leaving behind."

Trange' couldn't resist adding her own farewell: "Hope you drop the soap while you're in there." Her voice carried the satisfaction of someone who'd survived his schemes and lived to mock their failure.

Shaniece gave both women disapproving looks that carried more affection than actual censure. Despite their fractured relationships and philosophical differences, they'd stood by her when it mattered most. Their presence in this moment of victory meant more than they could possibly understand.

As law enforcement led Dalvin away to begin serving consequences he'd earned through months of evil choices, Shaniece watched through corridor windows until he disappeared from view. This chapter of her life was ending with justice served and new beginnings promising hope that seemed impossible just weeks earlier.

Thank You, Lord, she prayed as his figure vanished into custody, for turning even the darkest schemes into instruments of Your ultimate good. Help me build something beautiful from the ashes of what was destroyed.

CHAPTER 19: THE BREAKING POINT AND THE BREAKTHROUG

It's time to mend these friendships and restore our sisterhood, Shaniece thought as she fastened her pearl earrings, preparing for what might be the most important gathering of her life. The elegant dining room at Ché Pierre would typically host such meetings, but Renee had stopped answering calls from everyone except Trange'—a development that alarmed them all.

Downstairs in the parlor, Trange' waited with uncharacteristic patience, her transformation over recent weeks nothing short of remarkable. What had begun as reluctant acceptance of Shaniece's invitation to Bible study had evolved into genuine spiritual seeking. Their nightly prayer calls had become sacred time that bridged philosophical differences with shared vulnerability before God.

The hostage ordeal had fundamentally changed Trange'. Sitting mere feet from where she'd been bound and threatened, she found herself silently praying for peace despite the traumatic memories. The walls she'd built through years of survival were slowly crumbling as she recognized that what she'd been seeking through worldly success might only be found through divine connection.

Lord, she prayed quietly, I know I'm still learning this faith walk but help me be the friend these women need today. Help me build bridges instead of burning them.

Her journey from Octavia Shanika Burns—the foster child who'd clawed her way out of poverty—to Trange' Moreau had required constructing barriers that protected her from pain while isolating her from authentic relationships. The manufactured sophistication had been armor against a world that seemed designed to destroy people like her.

Now she understood that her friction with Shaniece had been rooted in an envious assumption that success came easily to someone born into privilege. Recent events had revealed the struggles, losses, and divine dependence that actually sustained her friend's strength.

I need to go to the same Source, she realized, and support her in the process rather than competing with her.

When Shaniece appeared at the top of the cascading staircase, Trange' looked up with new appreciation. The secret admiration she'd harbored—tinged with righteous envy—was transforming into genuine respect for a woman who'd chosen faith over bitterness despite having every reason for revenge.

"I hope Renee shows up." Apprehension gripped Trange's voice.

"I'm not sure," Shaniece replied honestly. "Don't get your hopes too high. She's been through trauma that changes people in ways we can't always predict."

They departed for what might be their last attempt at salvaging relationships that had sustained them for decades.

The sophisticated atmosphere of Mr. B's Bistro provided the perfect backdrop for conversations requiring both privacy and comfort. Located on the corner of Royal and Iberville Streets, the restaurant was renovated to look as if Hurricane Katrina had never touched it. The dark wood and etched glass created an environment more conducive to healing rather than confrontation.

Samantha and Coko had already claimed a corner table, their animated discussion pausing as Moni joined them, followed shortly by Shaniece and Trange' walking together—a sight that drew curious glances from their assembled friends.

"Well, this is unexpected," Samantha observed with a smile that mixed surprise with approval. "When did you two become prayer partners?"

"It's been developing over the past few weeks," Shaniece explained, settling into her chair while Trange' took the seat beside her—positioning that would have been impossible months earlier.

"Bible study and nightly prayers," Trange' added with self-deprecating humor. "Who would have thought I'd become one of those Christians who actually talks to God regularly?"

The transformation was evident in more than her words—her posture carried less aggression, her voice held warmth instead of perpetual defensiveness, and her eyes reflected peace that material success had never provided.

Before they could fully explore this unexpected development, Trange's phone buzzed with a text message that immediately commanded her attention.

"Renee's here," she announced, though her expression suggested the message contained more than a simple arrival notification.

"Before she comes in," Trange' said quickly, her voice carrying the urgency of someone delivering crucial intelligence, "I need you to understand where Renee is emotionally. She feels abandoned by this sisterhood, especially during her divorce crisis while everyone rallied around Shaniece's ordeal."

The accusation hit the table like a physical blow. Multiple voices rose in simultaneous protest—disbelief mixing with hurt that their loyalty could be questioned.

"That's not fair," Moni said with diplomatic authority she rarely displayed. "Renee has always maintained private boundaries. When we discovered her situation, events were already in motion. After two decades of friendship, we hoped she'd trust us enough to share her struggles before they reached crisis level."

"Exactly," Samantha interjected with conviction. "We can't support someone who won't let us into their pain until it explodes publicly."

Trange' felt a familiar fire rising in her chest—the defensive anger that had characterized her responses for years. But something different happened this time. Instead of launching a counterattack, she paused, breathed, and remembered recent prayer sessions about choosing peace over proving points.

"I hear what you're saying," she replied, her tone softening with effort that surprised everyone present. "And I apologize for my initial reaction. But I think we need to consider that our Renee was suffering in silence, and sometimes suffering people can't ask for help the way we think they should."

The response demonstrated growth that months of spiritual discipline were producing—ability to acknowledge multiple perspectives without abandoning loyalty to wounded friends.

"Regardless of fault," Coko added with wisdom that cut through defensive positions, "we owe her recognition of her pain and willingness to rebuild trust that may have been damaged."

"I'm not sure apologies will be sufficient," Trange' warned, though her voice carried sadness rather than satisfaction. "This new version of Renee is ... hardened. Bitter in ways that scare me."

Shaniece's disapproving glance reminded Trange' that spiritual growth included controlling her tongue, even when speaking truth.

"Okay, okay," Trange' conceded. "But it's accurate. The woman walking through that door isn't the same person who used to bring homemade cookies to our gatherings."

Storm Clouds Gathering

Renee entered the restaurant carrying atmospheric darkness that seemed to precede hurricanes. Her movements were sharp, deliberate, lacking the warmth that had once characterized her interactions with people she loved. Designer sunglasses hid eyes that might reveal too much vulnerability, while her posture suggested someone prepared for battle rather than reconciliation.

"Hello," she offered with mechanical politeness, removing her sunglasses to reveal eyes that held a mixture of pain, anger, and something approaching contempt.

Without waiting for responses, she signaled the waitress. "I need a drink. Something strong."

"Renee, I was just telling everyone about—" Trange' began, seeking to bridge immediate tension.

"Let me get my drink first," Renee interrupted with finality that brooked no argument. "Y'all continue with your sister-sister talk."

She pulled out her phone and began scrolling with attention that excluded everyone at the table—a digital barrier against unwanted emotional connection.

Trange' felt a familiar irritation rising. "Girl—"

"It's fine," Shaniece intervened quickly, placing a restraining hand on Trange's arm. "Let's give her space to process."

"Maybe she needs some Midol," Trange' muttered under her breath, earning a sharp nudge from Shaniece.

"What? God ain't finished with me yet," she defended.

"Keep talking and I will be," Renee shot back without looking up from her phone, proving that she'd been listening despite the appearance of disengagement.

"Oh, she speaks," Trange' replied with theatrical surprise, clapping her hands.

"When I want to," Renee snapped, scanning the room for their delayed server. "Where is my drink?"

The waitress arrived bearing Renee's order—a smoked old fashioned with blood orange that matched the bitter atmosphere she'd brought to their gathering. She nursed the drink with deliberate slowness while her friends watched uncertainly, unsure whether to proceed with attempted reconciliation or retreat from the obvious hostility.

After several sips, Renee looked up to find five faces studying her with expressions that mixed love with concern, hope with apprehension. The attention triggered something deeper than irritation—recognition that these women still cared despite her attempts to push them away through antagonistic behavior.

But caring wasn't enough to heal wounds that had festered in isolation. The anger she felt wasn't directed solely at them—it encompassed her ex-husband, the legal system that had failed her, the God who'd allowed her marriage to crumble, and the world that seemed designed to punish women who trusted too deeply.

They think they can fix this with apologies and girl talk, she thought bitterly. They have no idea what I've been through or how much their absence cost me when I needed them most.

The stage was set for confrontation that would either destroy their sisterhood completely or forge something stronger through honest acknowledgment of pain that silence had allowed to poison everything they'd once shared.

CHAPTER 20: LEGACY OF GRACE

Renee sat there like a powder keg, ready to explode. Over the past year, she had endured humiliation and personal destruction that would have broken weaker souls. The man she had loved—cherished, honored, and supported—had abandoned her in the most devastating way imaginable.

It wasn't simply that Marvin had left her for someone else. She could have processed an affair with another woman, though it would have wounded her deeply. She had no issues with homosexuality as an orientation—love was love, and people's hearts belonged where they belonged. But the deception that had poisoned the foundation of their marriage, the lies that had corrupted every sacred moment they'd shared, the realization that her entire adult life had been built upon his elaborate performance—that was what had shattered her world beyond recognition.

The moment she discovered the truth about her marriage, she began questioning her faith. And the moment she started questioning her faith, her world as she knew it began to crumble like ancient parchment exposed to flame.

But why didn't her sisters see this happening?

Yes, she had walked around polished, never showing too much emotion, maintaining the façade of the perfect wife and first lady. She wore her white pearls and oversized hats with dignity. She owned a reputable business that employed dozens of people in their community. She displayed what the Good Book defined as the virtuous woman—she fasted regularly, studied Scripture faithfully, and demonstrated what a woman of the church should embody.

And her reward for this devotion? For her husband to step out on her with a *man*, ultimately embarrassing her before the very congregation she had helped build, within the social circles she had cultivated through decades of careful relationship-building. For him to walk away seemingly unscathed while she remained to suffer the destruction his actions had wrought upon everything she held sacred.

What kind of cruel God did she serve?

Moni looked at her friend with eyes that reflected both love and regret. "I know words alone cannot heal what you've experienced. But I—and every one of your sisters right here—want to tell you how deeply sorry we are for everything that has happened, and how we failed to support you adequately during your greatest time of need."

They all turned their attention toward her, their faces radiating beams of love directed at her wounded heart. The anger that roared inside her clashed violently with the love being offered—two opposing forces creating internal warfare that threatened to tear her apart.

She scoffed bitterly. "Sisters."

Coko chimed in with gentle firmness, "Yes, sisters. Yes, family. Not a *perfect* family—imperfect human beings who make terrible mistakes. But we love you deeply, and we also acknowledge that we failed you when you needed us most."

She paused, her voice growing stronger with conviction. "Whatever anger you need to express, we'll absorb it. Whatever pain you need to release, we'll witness it. Tell us how we should have shown up for you, and what we can do going forward to help carry this burden with you instead of leaving you to bear it alone."

In that moment—that precise, sacred moment—Renee had to make a choice. She could continue holding onto the anger, hurt, and secrecy that had created this chasm between them, or she could risk vulnerability one more time with people who had proven themselves imperfect but present.

It started with one tear escaping from her eye, betraying her internal commandment that there would be no tears shed, no weakness displayed. Then there were two tears, then four, multiplying until they became streams coursing down her cheeks. Within seconds, uncontrollable floodgates of grief burst open as she sobbed without restraint.

"Let it all out," Samantha commanded with authority born of love, each woman rising from her chair to embrace their fallen sister.

The restaurant was sparsely attended, so there was no spectacle, no audience for her breakdown except the women who had earned the right to witness her pain. Renee released floodgates of hurt through her tears while no one judged, no one spoke unnecessary words, no one attempted to fix what needed to be felt before it could heal.

Tears stained high-fashion garments, mascara streaked carefully applied makeup, but no one cared about appearances. What mattered in that moment was healing through the sacred act of witnessed grief.

One by one, each woman succumbed to their own emotions and wept with their sister—not from empathy alone, because they couldn't fully comprehend the scope of what she'd endured, but because they cried for the hurt their sister was experiencing, the isolation she had suffered, and their own failure to prevent it.

Seconds stretched into minutes, and the minutes multiplied like the tears themselves. But as with any emotional downpour, the intensity eventually subsided.

Renee lifted her head, her voice barely above a whisper. "I don't know how I can come back from this." She gazed forward, looking beyond them as if seeing into a future she couldn't envision.

"We had the perfect life—three beautiful children, respected positions as pastor and first lady. We embodied everything about Black excellence and Christian leadership. And that man..." Her voice cracked with fresh pain. "I sacrificed everything for his success. I reduced myself so that he could rise. I played in the background so that he could shine. I went without so that he could have everything he desired."

She took a significant swig of her drink, liquid courage for confessions she'd never spoken aloud.

"I wasn't totally fulfilled in our marriage, but I honored our vows because that man was my husband, my family, my covenant partner before God." Another pause, another sip. "And you know what he left me with as his parting gift?"

The question hung in the air like a sword about to fall.

"HPV, which developed into cervical cancer." Her laugh held no humor—only bitter irony. "While he was out sowing his wild oats and having unprotected encounters, he gave me a sexually transmitted disease that transformed into something that could have been a death sentence."

She chuckled again, the sound hollow and haunting. "He always used to say I was his 'black Barbie.' I had no idea he really wanted a blonde Ken instead."

The women gasped audibly. They had known about the blonde, blue-eyed young man who had stolen Marvin's heart, but

STDs and *cancer?* This revelation added layers of cruelty they hadn't imagined possible.

"We didn't know," Trange' whispered, her voice thick with horror and compassion.

Renee took another deliberate sip. "No, you didn't know. But God knew. He watched that man abandon me and our three sons to pursue his authentic self, leaving me with a disease that threatens my life and my ability to provide for our children."

Her voice rose with anguish. "How am I supposed to care for three young men who need their father, whose mother has cancer? This was not the life I signed up for when I said 'I do' before God and witnesses. This cannot be the reality I'm supposed to accept."

The totality of the situation settled heavily on her friends' shoulders. There had been no obvious warning signs, nothing they could have detected or prevented. Each woman recognized that Renee's anger toward them existed primarily because of proximity—she needed someone to lash out against, and the pastor who had caused this devastation was no longer available as a target.

Understanding that sometimes relationships require us to serve as emotional sounding boards for those we love, they prepared themselves to absorb whatever pain she needed to release.

Moni stood and walked toward Renee, lifting her head to make direct eye contact. "Whatever you need, we are here for you. I want you to know—it may be difficult for you to receive this right now—but God still loves you."

Her voice gained strength as she continued. "We have witnessed firsthand the power of God and His ability to move mountains in impossible situations. We know there is purpose in our pain, even when we can't see it through our tears."

She gestured toward the other women. "I speak for myself and these other ladies when I say we're going to stand in the gap and continue interceding for you and your family. We're going to trust and believe that God will provide healing for your body, strength for your spirit, and restoration for your future."

Recognizing that these words might sound hollow given Renee's current spiritual crisis, Moni accepted the risk of rejection while offering hope anyway.

Each woman began sharing inspirational words of encouragement and concrete promises of continued support. They pulled out their phones to add her medical appointments to their calendars, ensuring they could all be present to champion and rally behind her throughout her treatment journey. Thus, they demonstrated through actions rather than just words, what true sisterhood looked like.

Renee made eye contact with Shaniece, her voice soft with regret. "I owe you an apology. You went through so much hell with Dalvin, and I was too caught up in my own world to—"

"You have absolutely nothing to apologize for," Shaniece interrupted with gentle firmness. "We have both walked through storms that threatened to destroy us."

She leaned forward, her voice carrying the authority of someone who had emerged from her own dark night of the soul. "But I can tell you with certainty that joy comes in the morning. When we hear that Scripture, we often think we can go to sleep and wake up the next day with everything magically resolved. But morning comes after the night—and night represents seasons of darkness and testing."

Her eyes held compassion earned through personal suffering. "Once this storm of darkness passes—and it will pass—the light will come into your life again, Renee. Joy—unspeakable joy—will arrive in God's perfect timing. You owe me no apology but know that nothing you could do would make me stop loving you. You are my sister, and I love you completely."

Tears began flowing from all the women at the table again as they stood and embraced each other in a circle of restored sisterhood.

Samantha caught the waitress's attention and ordered a bottle of Cabernet Sauvignon for the table. "I don't know about y'all, but I need something stronger than coffee after all this emotion," she joked, lightening the atmosphere while honoring the sacred space they'd just shared.

"What are we toasting to?" Coko asked, raising her glass.

"Sisterhood," Trange' declared without hesitation.

"Sisterhood," Renee agreed, lifting her glass with the first genuine smile she'd displayed all evening.

"Sisterhood," echoed Coko, then Moni, then Samantha.

Shaniece raised her glass last. "To sisterhood ... because my baby girl is going to need all of her aunties."

She touched her glass to her lips and then set it down gently.

Confusion and stunned expressions streaked across every face at the table.

"Aunties?" "Did she just say baby girl?" Comments echoed across the table like overlapping waves of shock and excitement.

Shaniece looked directly at Renee, her smile radiant with joy. "God is still in the blessing business." She touched her belly reverently. "I'm pregnant with a baby girl. You're all going to be aunties—every single one of you. So, we need to get our sisterhood back together and keep it strong, because if Baby Shaniece is anything like her mama, she's going to need all of y'all."

Joyful Chaos

The women erupted in celebration, demanding details about how this miracle had happened after doctors had declared conception impossible. They embraced and wept again—this time from pure joy and amazement at God's perfect timing.

"Man, I need some food," Samantha exclaimed, the emotional rollercoaster having worked up her appetite.

"Not before the mother-to-be gets fed," Moni protested protectively.

"I could be pregnant too," Samantha shot back playfully.

"Where's that engagement ring then?" Trange' challenged with renewed sass.

"Mind your business—that's between me and God," Samantha retorted, causing all of them to dissolve into laughter that washed away the last remnants of tension and pain.

They were sisters again—imperfect, wounded, but committed to walking through whatever storms life might bring, together rather than alone. And now they had a baby girl to anticipate, a new generation to love and protect and guide into understanding the power of authentic sisterhood.

God's timing, they were learning, was always perfect—even when it arrived through tears and looked nothing like what they had expected.

CHAPTER 21: FULL CIRCLE

The Sacred Sisterhood

The waiting room at Ochsner Cancer Center had become their second home over the past month. What had started as moral support for Renee's appointments had evolved into something deeper—a weekly pilgrimage where five women gathered to wage spiritual warfare against disease while building bonds stronger than blood.

Shaniece adjusted her position in the uncomfortable plastic chair, her hand instinctively moving to her still-flat stomach where life was quietly taking shape. At twenty weeks, the pregnancy remained their closely guarded secret, shared only among the sisterhood and her mother. But each day brought new awareness of the miracle growing within her—a gift she'd been told was impossible, arriving at the moment when her faith needed tangible evidence of God's restorative power.

"Renee Williams," the nurse called, clipboard in hand.

"We're coming too," Samantha announced, rising with the authority of someone who'd appointed herself chief advocate. The medical staff had learned not to argue with the five-woman army that accompanied their patient to every appointment.

As they walked down the sterile hallway, Moni's phone buzzed with a text from her husband. "Marcus says the kids are having a blast. Your boys are teaching his girls how to play basketball, and apparently they're all planning some elaborate fort in the backyard."

"Good," Renee smiled—an expression that came more frequently now, supported by the knowledge that her sons weren't facing this crisis alone. "Maybe they'll wear themselves out enough to actually sleep tonight."

Coko laughed. "David says the same thing. He's threatening to put them all to work in his garden if they have too much energy left over."

The integration of their families had happened naturally, organically, as if their children had been waiting for permission to become the cousins they were meant to be. Sleepovers rotated between houses, homework became group projects, and three boys grieving their father's abandonment found themselves surrounded by father figures who stepped into the gap without being asked.

"Dr. Harrison will see you now," the nurse announced, leading them into the consultation room where hope and fear danced together in fluorescent lighting.

Three hours later, they emerged from the medical center with news that defied statistical probability. Renee's latest scans showed significant reduction in tumor size—results that made her oncologist use words like "remarkable" and "unprecedented response to treatment."

"I'm not saying it's gone," Dr. Harrison had cautioned, "but whatever you're doing—meditation, prayer, lifestyle changes—keep doing it. Your body is responding in ways we don't typically see at this stage."

They'd looked at each other knowingly. Prayer wasn't just something they were doing; it was the foundation of everything they were building together.

"Celebration dinner?" Trange' suggested as they walked toward the parking garage. "I know a place that serves the best—"

"Actually," Shaniece interrupted, checking her watch, "I have an appointment I can't miss. But y'all go ahead. We'll celebrate properly this weekend."

Samantha's eyebrows rose with curiosity. "What appointment is more important than celebrating Renee's good news?"

"One that's been three months in the making," Shaniece replied cryptically. "Trust me, you'll understand soon enough."

The Mother's Wit

Her childhood home welcomed her with familiar scents—vanilla candles, fresh flowers, and the lingering aroma of her mother's famous cornbread. Walking through these rooms where she'd learned to pray, to dream, to believe in possibilities bigger than her circumstances, felt like returning to sacred ground.

"Baby girl," her mother called from the kitchen, "I've been praying all morning about this conversation we're about to have."

Eleanor Lincoln had aged gracefully into her seventies, her silver hair crowned like wisdom earned through decades of faithful living. But her eyes held the same sharp intelligence that had built a successful catering business while raising a daughter who would surpass every dream she'd dared to envision.

"Mama, before we start," Shaniece said, settling into the breakfast nook where she'd eaten countless meals and received immeasurable life lessons, "I need you to know that your granddaughter is going to be blessed with the most praying grandmother in Louisiana."

Eleanor's hands flew to her chest, tears immediately springing to her eyes. "Granddaughter? Oh, sweet Jesus, you're having a girl?"

"A girl who's going to need her grandmother's wisdom about how to rise above the circumstances of her conception and the character of her biological father."

The weight of that statement settled between them like morning fog—beautiful but requiring navigation with care and wisdom.

Eleanor reached across the table, grasping her daughter's hands with strength that had sustained them through every crisis they'd faced together. "Baby, let me tell you something about legacy that I learned from my own mama, and she learned from hers."

Her voice carried the authority of generational wisdom passed down through strong women who'd survived slavery, reconstruction, Jim Crow, and every attempt to destroy their families' foundation.

"Legacy isn't about the blood that flows through your veins—it's about the love that flows through your heart. That baby girl isn't being defined by Dalvin's DNA; she's being shaped by your faith, your character, your choices, and the village of love we're going to build around her."

She paused, allowing the truth to become deeply rooted.

"Every child born into this world carries two possibilities—they can become a product of their worst inheritance, or they can become proof of God's redemptive power. Which one she becomes depends on the love, guidance, and spiritual foundation we provide."

Shaniece felt tears gathering as her mother's words washed over wounds she didn't even realize still needed healing.

"But Mama, what if she asks about her father? What if she wants to know why he's not—"

"Then you tell her the truth appropriate for her age," Eleanor interrupted with gentle firmness. "You tell her that sometimes people make choices that hurt the people who love them most. You tell her that God can use even broken beginnings to create beautiful stories. And you tell her that she was wanted, prayed for, and celebrated from the moment you knew she existed."

Eleanor stood and moved to the window overlooking the garden where three generations of Lincoln women had found peace in growing things.

"You know what else you tell her? You tell her about forgiveness—not the kind that excuses bad behavior, but the kind that frees you from carrying other people's choices as your own burden. You teach her that forgiveness isn't about the person who hurt you; it's about the person you're choosing to become."

The Difficult Conversation

The drive to FaLessia's house felt longer than the actual distance, each mile weighted with uncertainty about how this conversation would unfold. Despite sharing a surname for fifteen years, she and Dalvin's sister had never developed the close relationship that marriage typically creates between women.

FaLessia had always been the religious one, the social worker, the woman who dedicated her life to serving others while Shaniece built business empires. Their differences had created polite distance rather than genuine sisterhood—a dynamic that needed to change for the sake of the baby who would need every available source of love and stability.

The modest house in Algiers reflected FaLessia's values—small but immaculate, with a garden that spoke of someone who found God in growing things and a porch that welcomed anyone seeking rest from life's storms.

"Shaniece," FaLessia greeted her with surprise that quickly transformed into warmth. "What brings you to my side of the river?"

"A conversation that's overdue by about fifteen years," Shaniece replied honestly. "Can we sit and talk? *Really* talk?"

They settled on the front porch where evening air carried the scent of jasmine and the distant sound of children playing in neighboring yards—a domestic symphony that provided the perfect backdrop for discussions about family, forgiveness, and the future.

"FaLessia, I need you to know something before anyone else does," Shaniece began, her hands unconsciously moving to her stomach. "I'm pregnant. You're going to be an aunt."

The silence that followed felt eternal. FaLessia's face cycled through multiple emotions—shock, joy, confusion, and something that might have been concerning.

"Pregnant?" she whispered. "But the doctors said—how is that even possible?"

"God's timing, apparently. Twenty weeks along, due in late spring."

FaLessia's expression shifted as the implications began crystallizing. "Does Dalvin know?"

"No, and he won't. At least not from me." Shaniece's voice carried finality that left no room for argument. "This baby deserves better than a father who chose drugs, violence, and criminal activity over his family. She deserves protection from his influence until she's old enough to make her own choices about any potential relationship."

"She?" FaLessia's voice cracked with emotion.

"Your niece. Who's going to need an aunt who can teach her about the good parts of her father's family legacy while protecting her from the destructive patterns that consumed him."

The Sister's Response

FaLessia stood abruptly, pacing to the porch railing where she gripped the painted wood with hands that trembled slightly. When she turned back, her face reflected internal war between family loyalty and moral conviction.

"Shaniece, I need you to understand something," she began, her voice gaining strength with each word. "What my brother did to you—the violence, the betrayal, the criminal behavior—I *cannot* and *will not* defend any of it. I've spent months praying for him, hoping for his redemption, but I refuse to enable his destruction by making excuses for inexcusable actions."

Her eyes blazed with righteous anger that surprised them both.

"He had everything—a wife who loved him, a successful practice, respect in the community, a family legacy of faith and service. And he threw it all away for what? Street drugs and criminal associates? Violence against the woman who'd stood by him through everything?"

She shook her head with disgust that went soul-deep.

"That's not the brother I raised. That's not the man our parents taught us to be. That's someone I don't recognize and frankly don't want to claim as family anymore."

The admission seemed to surprise FaLessia herself, as if she hadn't realized how completely she'd separated herself from the brother she'd once adored.

"But that baby," she continued, her voice softening with wonder, "that baby represents hope. Redemption. The possibility that God can give us beauty for ashes and create new legacies from broken foundations."

She returned to her seat, leaning forward with intensity that commanded attention.

"I want to be her aunt—not just in name, but in action. I want to teach her about prayer, about service, about using whatever gifts God gives her to bless other people. I want to show her that the Shaw family name can represent something beautiful instead of something shameful."

Tears began flowing down her cheeks as the full weight of the moment settled over her.

"And I want to thank you," she whispered, "for giving me the chance to be part of raising her. For not cutting me off because of what Dalvin did. For allowing our family name to continue through someone who might restore honor to it."

What followed was more than conversation—it was covenant-making. Two women who'd been connected by marriage but divided by differences now found common ground in their shared commitment to protecting and nurturing the life growing within Shaniece.

They discussed practical matters: how to maintain FaLessia's relationship with the baby while respecting Shaniece's boundaries about Dalvin's involvement. They planned holidays, birthdays, and traditions that would give their daughter a sense of extended family without exposing her to toxic influences.

But most importantly, they talked about legacy—the conscious choice to break generational cycles of dysfunction and replace them with patterns of faith, love, and service.

"I have one request," FaLessia said as the sun began setting over the Mississippi River. "When she's old enough to ask about her father, let me be part of that conversation. Not to defend him or make excuses, but to help her understand that people are complex—capable of both good and evil—and that she gets to choose which inheritance she claims as her own."

"And I have a request for you," Shaniece replied. "Help me raise a daughter who never doubts that she was wanted, planned for, and celebrated. Help me give her such a strong foundation of love that she never feels the need to seek validation from people who don't deserve her light."

They sealed their agreement with an embrace that felt like the beginning of true sisterhood—the kind that's chosen rather than inherited, built on shared values rather than shared DNA.

As Shaniece drove home through familiar streets that held so many memories of pain and triumph, she felt something she hadn't experienced in months: complete peace about the future. Her daughter would be born into a village of love that included a biological family who'd chosen to do better, chosen family who'd proven their loyalty through crisis, and a grandmother whose prayers had sustained multiple generations through every imaginable storm.

Thank You, Lord, she prayed silently, for taking the worst things that happened to me and using them to create the best possible foundation for her. Thank You for showing me that sometimes our greatest wounds become our children's greatest strengths.

The baby stirred slightly—the first movement Shaniece had felt—as if responding to her mother's prayers with confirmation that everything was going to be more than alright.

Everything was going to be blessed.

Dawn of New Beginnings

The morning sun painted Shaniece's balcony in shades of amber and rose gold, casting ethereal light across the wrought iron railings that overlooked gardens where ancient live oaks stood sentinel over her transformed world. She cradled her steaming cup of Belgian hazelnut coffee—the rich aroma mingling with jasmine-scented air that carried whispers of change and redemption.

A gentle breeze stirred the silk curtains behind her, causing them to dance like liturgical banners celebrating divine victory. The movement caught her kaftan, sending ripples through the flowing fabric as she swayed unconsciously, her body responding to nature's rhythm while her mind journeyed through the miraculous tapestry of the past six months.

Six months. Had it really been such a short time since her world had seemed to be crumbling beyond repair?

The criminal threats that had once kept her awake at night had evaporated like morning mist when Dalvin's associates turned on him with remarkable swiftness. Faced with federal charges and the prospect of decades in prison, they had offered his location and detailed testimony about his involvement in their operations in exchange for reduced sentences. Honor among thieves, it seemed, lasted only as long as personal freedom remained intact.

Under her strategic direction and Samantha's relentless execution, Hermosa Industries had not merely recovered—it had emerged stronger than ever. The $329 million settlement from Brooks, Bailey & Solomon had provided more than financial restoration; it had created opportunities for expansion that elevated the company to international prominence. New flagship stores had opened in Paris and Milan, their cosmetics line had secured exclusive contracts with luxury department stores across three continents, and their sustainable fashion initiative had garnered recognition from environmental organizations worldwide.

But perhaps most satisfying was their investment in FaLessia's nonprofit organization. The $5 million injection had transformed "God's Healing Hands" from a small community outreach into a comprehensive support system for at-risk families throughout Louisiana. They now operated transitional housing, job training programs, educational scholarships, and crisis intervention services that were changing generations of lives. Watching Dalvin's destructive legacy being redeemed through his sister's redemptive work felt like divine justice with a poetry that only God could orchestrate.

Her husband's deterioration had been swift and complete once his criminal associations were exposed. The man who had once commanded courtrooms with eloquent arguments had devolved into someone she barely recognized—hollow-eyed, desperate, begging for mercy from a justice system he had once manipulated. She had chosen not to attend his trial, though Samantha, Trange', and Renee had made certain they were present for every proceeding, serving as witnesses to consequences that natural justice demanded.

Partly, she couldn't bear to see the final destruction of someone she had once loved. But more importantly, she refused to be exposed to the stress and negativity that courtroom drama would have generated. The pregnancy had remained their closely guarded secret until a charity gala she'd hosted had made concealment impossible when her expanding figure could no longer be disguised by flowing evening gowns.

Since that revelation, Dalvin had been calling incessantly from his federal holding facility, desperate to connect, demanding rights he had forfeited through his choices.

A soft cry from inside the house interrupted her reverie, followed immediately by Trange's soothing voice offering comfort to the fussing infant.

"There's my baby!" Shaniece exclaimed as Trange' emerged onto the balcony carrying tiny Imani Kristina Shaw, her six-week-old daughter who had inherited her mother's delicate features and her grandmother Eleanor's expressive eyes.

The bundle of joy represented everything miraculous about God's timing—arriving healthy and perfect despite medical predictions that had declared conception impossible. Each tiny finger, every soft breath, served as tangible proof that divine plans supersede human limitations.

"Here, take Israel—he's getting fussy and wants his mama," Fa-Lessia announced as she joined them on the balcony, the morning sun creating a halo effect around her silver-streaked hair as she carefully transferred the squirming infant into Shaniece's waiting arms.

They traded babies with practiced ease—a routine that had developed over weeks of shared caregiving that had transformed obligatory family connections into genuine sisterhood.

God had blessed Shaniece with not just one miraculous child, but twins—Imani Kristina and Israel Kennedy Shaw. The double blessing had arrived after a pregnancy that defied every medical expectation, delivered safely despite concerns about her age and previous complications. Their births had strengthened her faith beyond measure and filled the emptiness that divorce had carved from her heart with joy so complete it sometimes overwhelmed her with gratitude.

Looking at her children—healthy, beautiful, wanted, and surrounded by love—she understood that wholeness didn't require a husband. It required alignment with God's purposes for her life, and these babies were undoubtedly part of that divine plan.

Israel settled immediately in her arms, his tiny fist grasping her finger with strength that belied his size. He possessed his father's strong jawline but his mother's gentle spirit, and she prayed daily that only the best genetic inheritance would manifest as he grew.

"Shaniece, it's time," FaLessia said gently, her voice carrying both encouragement and understanding of the difficulty ahead.

They moved into Shaniece's home office, where floor-to-ceiling windows offered commanding views of the Garden District while technology connected them to a federal correctional facility two hundred miles away. She settled into her executive chair with Israel in her arms while FaLessia positioned herself nearby with Imani, both babies peaceful in the presence of women who had already proven their devotion.

Taking a deep breath that carried prayers for wisdom, grace, and protection for her children's emotional well-being, Shaniece clicked the Zoom meeting link that would connect her babies to their biological father for the first time.

She focused on summoning a smile—not for Dalvin's sake, but for her children's future. Whatever happened in this conversation would become part of their story, and she was determined that their first meeting with their father would be marked by dignity rather than bitterness.

The screen flickered to life, revealing Dalvin in orange prison attire that stripped away every vestige of the successful attorney he had once been. The man staring back at her looked older, hollow, diminished by consequences that had reduced him to a number in the federal prison system.

But when he saw the babies, something shifted in his expression—a recognition of innocence that transcended his own guilt, love that existed despite his capacity for destruction.

"FaLessia, would you handle the introductions?" Shaniece requested, knowing that his sister's presence would provide an emotional buffer while ensuring the children's needs remained primary.

"Dalvin," FaLessia began, her voice carrying authority earned through years of social work with damaged families, "I want you to meet your children. This is Imani Kristina—your daughter. She's six weeks old, healthy, and already showing signs of her mother's intelligence."

She adjusted the camera angle so Dalvin could see Imani's sleeping face, tiny features peaceful in her aunt's protective embrace.

"And this is Israel Kennedy—your son. He's got your stubborn streak but his mother's gentle heart, thank God."

Dalvin's composure shattered completely. Tears streamed down his face as he pressed closer to the screen, desperate to bridge the physical distance that his choices had created.

"They're beautiful," he whispered, his voice breaking with emotion that seemed to surprise him with its intensity. "They're absolutely perfect."

His eyes found Shaniece through the camera. "Thank you. I know I don't deserve this. I know I forfeited any right to see them when I chose drugs and crime over my family. But thank you for giving me this chance."

"I didn't want to do this," Shaniece replied honestly, her voice gentle but firm. "But I felt God pushing me to allow this connection. As the Scripture says, 'not my will, but Thy will be done.'

Maybe seeing them will provide the motivation you need to truly change your life."

Dalvin leaned forward, speaking directly to the camera as if addressing his children. "Imani, Israel, I promise you—I swear on everything I have left—that I'm going to turn my life around. I'm going to become the father you deserve, even if it takes fifteen years for me to hold you."

His voice gained strength with conviction that sounded more authentic than anything Shaniece had heard from him in years.

"I won't let you down again. When I get out of this place, I'm going to spend the rest of my life proving that you can be proud to carry my name."

The call concluded with promises that only time would prove genuine, but Shaniece felt peace about providing this opportunity for connection. Whether Dalvin followed through on his vows remained to be seen, but she had obeyed the divine prompting to offer grace where condemnation would have been easier.

Evening at Ché Pierre

FaLessia had taken the twins for their evening routine, giving Shaniece the opportunity to reconnect with her sisters at their traditional gathering place. As her Mercedes pulled into the familiar circular drive, she felt anticipation building for this celebration of how far they'd all traveled together.

Ché Pierre had outdone itself for their private dining experience. The main restaurant had been transformed into something approaching royal grandeur—crystal chandeliers cast prismatic light across tables adorned with French silk linens and fresh orchid centerpieces. Gilded mirrors reflected candlelight that danced across walls hung with original Impressionist paintings on loan from private collectors who owed Renee' professional favors.

The maître d' had arranged their seating in the alcove where floor-to-ceiling windows overlooked the courtyard garden, creating an intimate atmosphere that encouraged authentic conversation while providing a visual feast that spoke to their elevated circumstances and refined tastes.

As Shaniece approached their table, she heard familiar laughter and spirited conversation—no tension, no underlying conflict, only the easy communion of women who had weathered storms together and emerged stronger for the experience. Well...with Trange' present, there might still be occasional moments of sass, but even her sharp edges had been softened by grace.

She paused before joining them, taking a moment to truly see each woman and marvel at the transformations that had occurred in their lives.

The Evolution of Sisters

Trange' sat with a posture that radiated confidence tempered by humility—a remarkable change from the defensive aggression that had once characterized her interactions. Her newfound devotion to God was evident in more than Sunday church attendance; she now participated in every Bible study, arrived early for prayer meetings, and had even begun teaching financial literacy classes at FaLessia's nonprofit. She was still working on her temper, but now when provoked, she would smile sweetly and suggest that people "try Jesus and not me, because God ain't finished with me yet, but He is definitely working on my patience."

Renee glowed with vitality that defied her recent cancer battle. Her partnership with FaLessia in outreach and advocacy for single mothers had given her purpose that transcended personal pain while her catering business had expanded into event planning for nonprofit organizations throughout the Gulf South. Her three sons were thriving under the guidance of "uncles" Marcus and David, who had stepped into the fatherhood gap without being asked and with wholehearted commitment that spoke to their character.

Moni had surprised them all by discovering courage she never knew she possessed. Her decision to join the church choir had revealed vocal abilities that left congregations speechless and her friends stunned. When they'd attended her church debut, watching their quiet friend belt out notes that would have intimidated Tamela Mann or Tasha Cobbs, they'd realized that God had been preparing gifts in secret for public blessing.

Coko had channeled her natural wisdom into a writing career that was gaining national recognition. Her self-help book about discovering God's divine purpose had climbed bestseller lists while her follow-up manuscript about friendship and spiritual growth was generating publisher interest that promised financial independence. Her husband's unwavering support had enabled book tour opportunities that were spreading her influence far beyond Louisiana.

And Samantha—her rock, her business partner, her chosen sister—had been a force of nature in both personal support and professional excellence. The fashion line she was launching under Hermosa's umbrella, "House of Gracieux," represented her creative vision finally finding expression. Her inaugural runway show was scheduled for the following month, and every woman at this table would be participating: Trange' and Coko as models (Trange' had announced rather than asked her participation), Moni providing musical accompaniment, while Renee and Shaniece would occupy front row seats with baby Imani and Israel watching their aunties command the fashion world's attention.

The Toast of Sisterhood

As they settled into their evening of celebration, Coko rose with wine glass in hand, her author's gift for words preparing to capture the essence of what they'd all experienced.

"Ladies," she began, her voice carrying the same authority that had captivated readers across the country, "I want to toast not just our friendship, but our transformation. Six months ago, we were women carrying individual burdens that threatened to destroy us—Shaniece facing violence and betrayal, Renee battling cancer and abandonment, Trange' hiding behind walls that kept everyone at distance, Moni suppressing gifts that God intended for public blessing, Samantha channeling creativity into everyone else's success except her own, and me ... well, me trying to fix everyone else instead of pursuing my own calling."

She paused, allowing her words to settle while candlelight reflected in the tears beginning to gather in multiple eyes.

"But look at us now. Look at what God has done with our willingness to be vulnerable with each other, to show up imperfectly, to love through disagreement and support through crisis."

Her voice gained strength as she gestured toward each woman.

"Shaniece, you chose forgiveness over revenge and received blessings that exceeded your wildest dreams. Renee, you chose healing over bitterness and found purpose that transcends personal pain. Trange', you chose authenticity over performance and discovered faith that's transforming everything about how you move through the world. Moni, you chose courage over comfort and unleashed gifts that are blessing thousands. Samantha, you chose investment in others and created space for your own dreams to flourish."

She raised her glass higher, candlelight catching crystal and creating rainbows that danced across the ceiling.

"And all of us chose sisterhood over isolation, grace over judgment, and faith over fear. We proved that women supporting women isn't just a hashtag—it's a spiritual discipline that releases power we never knew we possessed."

The tears were flowing freely now, makeup be darned.

"So, I toast to the sisters—not perfect women, but women made perfect through love that covers multitudes of flaws. Not women who never fall, but women who help each other rise. Not women who have it all figured out, but women willing to figure it out together."

Shaniece couldn't agree more. Every word resonated with truth earned through trials that had tested but not broken bonds forged in divine purposes.

They all stood simultaneously, as if choreographed by Heaven itself, crystal glasses raised in celebration of friendship that had survived everything hell could unleash against it.

"To the sisters!" they declared almost in unison, the words echoing through Ché Pierre's elegant dining room before crystal met crystal in symphony of celebration.

As they settled back into their seats, beginning an evening of conversation that would stretch past midnight, Shaniece felt overwhelming gratitude for the journey that had brought them to this moment. Every betrayal, every loss, every moment of defeat had been working together for good that surpassed her ability to comprehend.

She was a single mother of twins, but she wasn't alone. She was a divorced woman, but she wasn't broken. She was a survivor of domestic violence, but she wasn't defined by victim status. She was a woman who had chosen faith over fear, forgiveness over revenge, and love over bitterness—and those choices had created a life more beautiful than anything she could have designed for herself.

Thank you, Lord, she prayed silently while her friends' laughter filled the air around her, for taking my broken pieces and creating a masterpiece that brings You glory and brings me joy.

The circle was complete. The sisterhood was restored. The future stretched brightly ahead with possibilities that only God could orchestrate.

And it was all very, *very* good.

ABOUT THE AUTHOR

Reverend because of God's leading. Doctor because of life's lessons...Introducing Dr. Mario DeSean Booker, the Doctor of Drama! Yes, he writes scholarly nonfiction, but he has another side...

In his debut urban fiction novel, Dr. Booker weaves a gripping narrative that tests the complexities of family, love, law, and loyalty. Set against the backdrop of the Big Easy, his characters navigate a world where love, betrayal, and power intersect in unexpected ways. With rich, multidimensional characters and a plot that keeps readers on the edge of their seats, this novel promises to be the first in a series that will captivate and inspire.

Does God have their backs? Get ready to dive into a world where the lines between honor and humanity blur, and where every twist and turn reveals deeper truths about our society. *Beauty for Ashes* is only the beginning—stay tuned for more thrilling adventures with these unforgettable characters!